MIRAGE

AGE

TRACY CLARK

Houghton Mifflin Harcourt
Boston   New York

For information about permission to reproduce selections from
this book, write to trade.permissions@hmhco.com or to Permissions,
Houghton Mifflin Harcourt Publishing Company, 3 Park Avenue,
19th Floor, New York, New York 10016.

www.hmhco.com

Text set in ITC Legacy Serif Std.
Book design by Sharismar Rodriguez

Library of Congress Cataloging-in-Publication Data is available.
ISBN 978-0-544-51790-5

Manufactured in the United States of America
DOC 10 9 8 7 6 5 4 3 2 1
4500597800

This book is dedicated to everyone who has ever bravely leaped into their fear and been altered by it. Fear is a transformative fire when you face it.
I salute your courage.

Death is a stripping away of all that is not you.
The secret of life is to "die before you die"—
and find that there is no death.

—Eckhart Tolle

ONE

IT'S MY JOB to open the jump door. I love the look on the first-timers' faces when the door slides open like a gaping mouth. Wind shoves its way into the cabin, elbowing through the rows of people sitting on the floor of the plane, their jaws so strained with nerves, they look like they could bite through a steel pipe. It's go time and they know it. The air slapping their faces makes it real.

When I open the door, it's crazy loud. To me, the blasting wind, the unending bowl of blue sky, screams *freedom*. But I think some of them hear a different voice than I do. Judging from their expressions, Death herself rides on the wind, whispering in their ears.

And yet they jump.

That's so sick. I know how they're gonna feel when they

touch ground. Badass. Superhuman. Nothing makes you feel more alive than giving Death the finger and having fun while you're doing it.

I kneel in the doorway and hang my head out into the wind to spot the drop zone, then signal the pilot. The engine immediately powers down from a roar to a satisfied purr. I smile at the petrified faces of the new jumpers as they lumber through the hollow cabin to the opening, take a beat to register the insanity of what they're about to do, and leap into their own fear. The air snatches them, pulling them away from the aircraft and from who they were before this moment.

The plane is nearly empty now, except for this one guy. He shuffles toward me and the open door with the distinct resistance of a man who's clearly not having fun. I remember him coming in this morning, all bravado and balls, to skydive for his twenty-first birthday. But now he looks like he might barf.

Our best jumpmaster, Paco, does the last-minute safety check of his equipment and gives the guy another quick run-through of the hand signals he'll need to follow if he doesn't want to die on his birthday.

"You forgot one!" I yell through the roar of wind.

Paco looks at me quizzically while the guy looks at Paco

in this terrified *How could you forget a hand signal? What in the hell am I doing trusting you with my life?* kind of way.

I raise my fist and shake it menacingly in the birthday boy's face. "Did he tell you what *this* means?" He swallows a wad of spit and terror but doesn't answer.

"It means, 'Do what he says or he'll beat you!'"

Paco laughs and shakes his head, but the scared guy just blinks as small beads of sweat form on his upper lip. I smile. Birthday Boy will jump. He can't be out-balled by a seventeen-year-old girl with Red Baron Snoopy on her jump helmet.

I blow them a kiss and fall backward out of the plane.

It's my favorite way to exit. Surrender into gravity. Baptism by air. It's cobalt summer sky, rushing wind, the scrubby expanse of the Mojave Desert, and . . . survival. It's pure. When I'm out here, nothing else exists.

I watch the guys leap from the jump door together before I tuck one arm under me to flip over and face the ground. Land is rushing at me, yes, but I don't feel the sensation of falling. I'm cradled, like I'm balancing on my stomach on a ball of air, flying.

I check my altimeter. Just dropped through seven thousand. There's still time to enjoy the ride before I have to pull my ripcord. The view never gets old. The desert stretches on forever, a big open palm with roads grooved across it like lifelines. The tail end of the Sierra Nevada is on my right, and a few pimply hills dot the flat land to the east. An occasional wisp of cloud rises past, reminding me how fast I'm falling.

Since I have no one out here with me, I play with my body, experimenting with the effects of small movements. The air is the opposite of land. Reach in front of me, and I move backward; pull my arms in, extend my legs, and I move forward. Relax my arch, and my body buffets a bit. People don't realize that skydivers aren't just falling. We're dancing with the current. Our movements are even more crucial when we jump with other people. A formation dive is like doing the tango . . . with twenty people at once . . . at 170 miles per hour.

I pull when I'm high enough to still enjoy some canopy time. My legs dangle from the harness like I'm a kid in a swing; then I press them together as I make my final turn into the wind and run out my landing in the large, flat circle of cleared sagebrush. There's enough of a light, heated breeze that I have to spin around and drop one toggle so my canopy won't fill with air, become a sail, and try to drag me across the desert.

The distinctive putt-putt sound of my parents' drop-zone golf cart bounces toward me, my cousin Avery behind the wheel. Her approach reminds me of when Dom and I were on his motorcycle and we had to totally alter course because we spotted a swarm of Mormon crickets advancing like a low red cloud.

I sigh with disappointment. My dad never comes out to get me. He does it for his "boys"—all the military guys with their faded Army Ranger caps with their Army "blood wings" pinned on the front who make the drop zone their second home. If you can't be in a combat zone, you might as well be skydiving, right? I think they're addicted to risk.

So what's my excuse? People always want to know why I nonchalantly do something that to them is inconceivable.

I'm addicted to the rush.

Avery doesn't jump, but she recently discovered she likes to hang out here. For a boy-crazy girl, a skydiving center is a very target-rich environment. She skids to a halt in the packed dirt, casting billowing clouds of copper dust around the tires and my feet. "I thought you had to work today," I say, a little breathless from my landing and the afternoon heat.

"Oh, I worked . . . until I didn't want to anymore. Then I claimed 'female issues.' My boss let me go faster than you can say 'superabsorbent.' He can't stand it when a woman brings up that she is, in fact, a woman."

"Most men can't," I answer. "My dad would give his remaining testicle to have had a boy instead of me."

"How many does that jump make?" she asks, quickly deflecting the topic of my dad's post-IED balls and saving me from how I sounded nine years old for a second there.

"Two sixty-eight." I've racked up a good number of jumps since I convinced my parents to sign for me when I reached legal jumping age last year. I argued for it on the grounds that it's not good business if you're not confident enough to let your own offspring jump. My dad shrugged indifferently and signed. My mother stared at me long and hard before shaking her head and mumbling something about destiny and that she has no control over how and when I die. "Death doesn't want me," I reassured her. "Too busy working for the government." The way Dad jerked his head up and scowled made me wish I'd kept my mouth shut.

I can't say anything right around him.

Birthday Boy intercepts us with his hair blown back all Einstein and rings around his eyes where his goggles indented his skin. He's smiling the broad smile of a man who is temporarily insane with his own superpowers.

"You are *so* drinking tonight," I predict, at which point he lets out a huge whooping yell and punches at the sky in triumph.

Avery grabs my arm, startled, and leans in. "He's positively primal."

"Yeah," I mumble, tugging impatiently at a corner of my chute that has snagged on a green ruffle of sagebrush. "Watch out for him, though. He's high on adrenaline. It's like twenty buckets of caffeine. For the next three hours he'll be invincible."

"Excellent," she says, fixing him with lowered lashes and a sideways look.

"Yeah, excellent. Until you'll find him curled up in the fetal position under a picnic table, sound asleep from the adrenaline crash."

"Or the whiskey."

"True that."

"You guys make it look all cool and thrilling, but normal people don't actually like jumping out of airplanes," Avery says.

"I make it a point *not* to be normal."

"Clearly. You're *you*. But something about humans pretending they can fly is a definite major violation of the rules of nature."

"Would we do it otherwise? Humans break rules to prove we can."

"Yeah, well," she says, "I could live my whole life without falling out of a plane, thanks."

I stop short of calling her a whuffo for hanging out here when she has no intention of ever jumping. But if she eyes my Dominix again with those lashes like she's eyeing Birthday Boy right now, it's on.

"Falling is the easy part. Trick is," I say, tapping her on the chest, "taking the leap."

Avery snorts, but not without some blend of admiration and incredulity in her eyes. "You're nuts."

"Oh, hell, yes." I pull the rest of my chute into my arms and climb aboard the golf cart. "I'd rather be crazy and fully alive than safe and half-dead."

TWO

THE DROP-ZONE HANGAR has its back to the westerly winds. It's open, with jumpers getting their rigs on for the next hop, riggers on the mats meticulously folding and packing chutes, and a couple of guys napping in lawn chairs. One has his mouth hanging open. It'll be a matter of minutes before someone shoots the air compressor in his piehole or glues his shoes to the floor.

Under the row of flags on the back wall, a large group of guys slide around the concrete floor on creepers, practicing their formation dive. Their bellies are on the boards, feet in the air, as they move and switch patterns. It's like synchronized swimming on wheels, only sweatier and with lots of laughing and swearing.

I dump my rig in a pile on the carpet and run over to the group, take a flying leap, and land on Dom's back. We roll across the floor, bounce into the wall, ricochet, and spin in a circle. All the while I hold on tight and kiss the back of his warm neck, burying my nose in his jet-black hair, which reminds me of rippling water at midnight.

"Now this is *my* idea of a tandem," Dom murmurs. He reaches behind him and squeezes my butt.

"Ryan Poitier Sharpe!" My mother's Caribbean accent cuts through the chatter in the hangar. I roll off Dom and sit on my knees. She stands right outside the hangar doors. Late-afternoon light glows behind her vivid flowered shirt and red head wrap. Her lips are color coordinated with the wrap and glowing like a stoplight against her smooth black skin. My mother is a hibiscus in the eternal beige of the desert.

I shrug the *what's up* shoulders and am met with a stern look. "Be right back," I whisper to Dom when she crooks her finger at me.

"I don't like to see that." She points vaguely in the direction of Dom and leads me to the office. "This is a public establishment. A business. *Our* business."

"He's my boyfriend, Mom. That's *my* business. We were just goofing around."

"Yes, but *must* you crawl all over each other in public like a couple of monkeys? It's unseemly."

I always laugh when Mom uses that word. It's a carryover

from growing up on Cat Island. *"Unseeeemly,"* I tease, imitating her island accent. Like clockwork, when I laugh, Mom laughs. And my mother doesn't just chuckle. Her laugh is full-bodied and carbonated. Her laugh is dark, sticky soda. We can never stay mad at each other.

She smacks me on the rear with her clipboard and shoos me out of her office as my father walks in. I touch his arm tentatively, but he slips away like an eel, busying himself with a pile of mail on the desk. I stare, trying to think of something to say to engage him. Dad slices the top of an envelope, shakes the letter open, and smiles broadly. It's the sun appearing from behind a curtain of clouds. The drop zone is the only place I ever see my dad's *real* smile. I stay because I want to know what's in the letter that has made it appear.

"The good news," he says, "is that we've made the short list of locations for the X Games."

"And the bad?" Mom asks, her painted nails resting on his shoulders.

He rubs his forehead. "If we don't get that event, our doors will close for good."

We all sigh. I knew things were tight, but I had no idea they were that critical. This place can't close. It's our life and the only thing holding Dad's PTSD in check. It keeps him focused on something other than his injuries, his losses, his bad dreams. His razor pain. "What do we have to do to make sure we get it?" I ask, squaring my shoulders in a *reporting for duty* kind of way.

My question brings his gunmetal gray eyes to meet mine. "We need to get their attention. We need a huge bigway when they come to scout the DZ — so many jumpers in the air that the formation will look like a spaceship landing. It'll take every experienced jumper we know to pull it off."

"I want in," I say, a pebble of hope lodging in my chest. When he shakes his head, I firmly tell him, "I'm ready."

"No," Dad answers in his first-sergeant voice while riffling through stacks of mail on his desk. "I assess your readiness. You're too young, too inexperienced, and this is too important. I need perfection. Absolute precision. It's not personal; it's business. Understand?"

"Yes, sir," I mumble, but it *is* personal. Do people have to be willing to die in order to earn his respect? Is having a penis a prerequisite for his regard? I back out of the office right into Dom's outstretched arms. He whispers in my ear, "Come with me. I've got something to show you."

Dom's motorcycle growls when he revs it, and he motions for me to climb on. I settle into the leather seat, wrapping myself around him. I love the feel of his hand cupping my outer thigh and the way my heart slams into my back when we take off. I have no idea where we're going, but he's bypassed the airport gate, so it would seem the mystery location is on the field somewhere.

Steel airplane hangars flash by in neat rows. It's like we're driving up the pages of a book: every sentence another row of evenly spaced hangars. Some are singles, some double wide for larger planes. They are uniformly imperfect. We turn left at the second to last row. This is the forgotten sector of the small municipal airport. In fact, the last time I was in this section was a year ago, to help my dad hang a new windsock. You know, the little things I'm qualified to do.

Dom cuts the engine and rolls to a stop in front of one of the larger hangars. He kickstands the bike and hops off. I slide forward into the warm space his body left on the seat and fondle the handlebars. "I want one so I can ride whenever I want."

"I got something you can ride." Dom's dimples are in the on position as he smiles playfully. I roll my eyes. "Come with me," he says with a gentle kiss to my nose.

I follow him to the side of the hangar where there's a regular door. Dom fishes a key from his jeans pocket and slides it in the keyhole.

"Whose hangar is this?" I ask.

"I found out from the airport manager that it's on the abandoned list. They're trying to locate the owners — some kind of ultrareligious nutjobs who leased the hangar and then just disappeared. The airport is trying to serve them an eviction notice because they haven't been paying." He pulls me into the dark hangar. "The contents will be auctioned off if they can't locate the owners. Until they do, it's our secret hideaway."

"Our secret hideaway smells like mice and dust," I say, crinkling my nose. As my eyes slowly adjust to the dim light, I see a large motor home filling the space behind Dom. It's covered with a powdery layer of grime, but it's obvious how nice the RV is. Metallic lavender and silver paint glints in the shaft of sunlight from the open door, which Dom moves to close. As he does, the triangle of light slinks back into the shadows, and we're left standing together in the hushed room with only an occasional airplane engine whirring outside.

Dom presses his lips against mine, reminding me of our first kiss and how it was not soft, but urgent and fiery. It was me who initiated it, but he denies that. He takes my hand and leads me up two small metal steps to the front door of the motor home. I don't know why my heart is racing at simply trespassing in an abandoned hangar, but I love it when my body hums with signals — excitement, danger, alarm. It's when these red flares shoot up inside me that I feel most alive.

"Who would dump an expensive RV like this and just vanish?" I ask, noting an extension cord snaking across the floor of the hangar. "You wired the power?" I ask, and Dom nods. He prepped our hideaway. Dom directs me inside with his hand on the small of my back. "I can't see a thing," I complain, reaching out in front of me into the blackness. My skin registers a drop in temperature, like the random, mystifying spots in lakes that are fifteen degrees colder. Goose bumps rise on my outstretched arms, and a wave of trepidation sweeps its rough hand down my spine.

A light switches on, and the RV is bathed in a yellow glow. I screech at my own reflection in the mirror in front of me and then bust out laughing.

Dom pokes my back. "Silly."

"Hey, I didn't expect to see someone standing there, even if that someone is me! Wow. This place is boss."

It's a miniature house on wheels, with a kitchen, a sofa, and an oak dining table with padded booth benches. I step farther inside. The dank smell of the hangar has disappeared. In its place rise the diminishing sharp odors of bleach and the chemical smell of new carpet. Dom watches as I open cabinets, check the fridge, flip switches. "This is camping in style," I say, clicking my fingernail against a row of dusty glasses that are hanging upside down in an overhead cabinet. They jangle against one another. "When we're older, let's rent one of these and drive all over hell and back."

"How 'bout I ride my bike, you follow me like my road crew and cook me dinner, and—"

"Screw that," I say with a raised eyebrow. "You be *my* road crew."

While the place has obviously been scrubbed clean of both use and the personality of the owners, my poking around reveals traces of a previous life. A case of some kind of nutrition drink sits unopened under the kitchen table. A maroon Bible stands lonely in a little magazine nook built into the end of the couch. I run my finger over the smooth gold crown of the pages, coating my finger with a film of dust, which I wipe on my shorts. The bathroom still has toilet paper on the roll and a stack of white towels — thin, like tea towels or hospital towels — folded in the cabinet under the sink. I slide them aside, knocking them into something, which falls sideways with a rattling sound.

It's a prescription bottle, totally full of morphine. That's some heavy-duty pain stuff. I wonder why it's full. Why was it left here? The urge to swipe the pills comes over me like a drive-by devil before I put them back and head down the narrow hallway and slide the door into its pocket. A queen bed fills the middle of the room and is surrounded by honey-colored cabinets. Blankets, sheets, and pillows are stacked on the mattress. I glance over my shoulder at Dom.

There's want in his eyes.

It's a certain look I've come to recognize: chin lowered a bit, eyes focused and penetrating. I love that look. But instead of coming toward me like I expect, he leans a shoulder against the wall and stares at me with his arms crossed.

Dom holds his ground when I think he'll advance. Surprises when I think he has no more mysteries. Six months ago, when I pegged him for another hotshot adrenaline junkie, he showed me poetry and tender pencil drawings of hawks, my profile, and his dead mother's strong hands making tortillas.

People don't always like Dom on first impression. For instance, my best friend, Joe. Well, Joe doesn't like him after many impressions. I don't know why. But to me, Dom is like the art he loves so much: complicated and nuanced. The more I look, the more beautiful he is. My heart inflates each day, expanding and rising up, up, and he holds the rope that tethers me when I feel like I'll float away. In turn, I do the same for him. We urge each other into wild explorations, then belay each other to reality.

Needing to kiss his lips right this second, I take the length of the hallway in two strides and grab his chin. Our lips melt together—powerful, moist fire. His mouth, his jaw, his tongue . . . he is everything hard and soft at once. I reach under his T-shirt and run my hand down his stomach toward the snap of his jeans. He stops my advances with a gentle hand on my collarbone.

He turns me around so I'm facing the full-length hall mirror and stands behind me. "Look at yourself," he whispers into my curls. His hand caresses my jaw with the sensitivity of a sculptor, and his thumb runs over my lips. "You're beautiful."

I'm not sure why I feel a foreign shyness when Dom says this. When he looks at me adoringly, I feel like a lone sunflower in a field, and he's the sun I arch toward. I feel truly *seen*. I'm not going to be falsely modest and say I don't know I'm attractive. Guys look. Hell, even girls look. But I think it's more because I'm interesting, with one foot in each parent's race.

Before she lost her sight, my grandmother said I was the combination of the smooth, dark rum of her beloved Caribbean and the imperious determination of a bank of white clouds marching over the land.

Gran has poetry in her.

I look in the mirror every day, but it's different when someone's with you. I look now to see what Dom sees. It's like meeting me for the first time. My reflection watches back. Stops me cold. I look different to myself. Slightly off. A shiver passes over my skin, raising the fine hairs on my arms. I stare hard into my own eyes. They look strange, intense, as if they are studying *me*—as if this reflection has been here in this motor home all along, waiting for me to look—and I'm unsettled enough to close my eyes.

Dom kisses my neck, and I shut the eerie image out, concentrating on the sensation of his lips soft against my skin, my earlobe. He nips my shoulder. "Don't close your eyes, Ry. Watch."

His hands grasp my hips—a possessive move that gives me chills—and then slide down the outside of my thighs. He brings them up again slowly, and we watch together as he runs them over my breasts, his fingers peeling my T-shirt up to expose my stomach. I love the contrast in browns when his olive Mexican hand slides over my darker island skin.

My breath comes faster as he undoes the button of my shorts. I look down at his tapered fingers brushing along the waistband, but he gently raises my chin back to our image. He inches my zipper down and slides his hand lower. I whisper, "Yes," because I want his hand in my pants more than anything at that moment.

I reach my arm back, seize his black hair, and tug. Dom growls softly and stares hard into my eyes in the mirror. He's right about this game. There's something about watching ourselves that heightens the experience. We are witnesses to our own beautiful, raging lives. I'm loving watching us until I catch my eyes again in the mirror, and a chilling thought hits me like a cold wind:

These eyes aren't mine.

THREE

MY EYES ARE dark, moist earth.

These other eyes—superimposed over mine—are the deep Arctic Ocean with ice marbling underneath. I shiver, pull Dom's hands from my skin, and turn away from the mirror, into his chest. "We'd better get back." I feel the foreign eyes on my spine, and the hairs rise on my neck and my stomach flutters with nerves.

"What? Noooo," he groans, sliding his hands down my arms. "That has, like, five kinds of rejection and suck written all over it."

I scoot out of his grasp. "My dad asked me to go up on the sunset jump," I lie, willing myself not to look at the mirror and the ghostly *otherness* within it.

Dom does an exaggerated package shift; whether it's for show or not, I don't know and don't care. I want to feel the sun on my back instead of phantom eyes. I leave him standing in the hall as I fling open the door and hop past the steps onto the concrete floor of the hangar. I'm outside before he's even turned off the light.

I can tell he's disappointed. He takes forever to lock the door. But when he turns toward me, his eyes crease with concern. "You okay?"

I slide onto his bike, trying to remember if I've ever been so creeped out. "I'll be okay if you let me drive us back."

"Woman—"

I turn the key and gas it. "You getting on back or walking?"

"I know better than to tangle with you when you have the tiger look."

"Hold on tight," I warn, and then suck in my breath when he hooks his fingers inside the inseam of my shorts.

"No fair!" I yell as I gun it so fast the front tire pops off the pavement and we lurch forward.

"I never object when you do it to me," he yells back. We both laugh into the wind.

"Dammit, I forgot to pack my chute from the last jump. I left it lying on the mat," I tell Dom as we pull up to the skydive center.

He slides off the bike, helps me with the kickstand, and kisses my forehead. "I'll pack it for you. I'm faster."

"Okay." I toss him his bike keys. "But you'd better not pack me for a hard opening like you did the other day."

"I was mad at you for flirting with that tool in the aviator glasses."

"I was not flirting with him!" I caress his wind-stung cheek. "You wanna go up?"

He wipes his eyes with both fists like a tired toddler. "Nah. I'd like to do one more practice session on the creepers before we try the new formation."

I wish he would jump with me this time. The image in the mirror has me unsettled, the sensation coating my skin and sinking in, infecting my spirit. I want Dom's hand in mine as we fly. But it's just as well. There's business to handle with my dad. Surely there's a way to change his mind about the big-way, and having Dom there will only make me look like I need him — which I don't.

My sneakers pound the desert sand as I jog into the hangar toward my parents' office. Dad's still behind his desk, talking on the phone. I fade into the wallpaper and wait until I'm acknowledged, like I've been trained to do. He hangs up and raises his eyebrows. "Yes?"

This is a man who appreciates directness, so I get to the

point. "I care about this place as much as you do. What can I do to convince you I'm ready for the big-way?"

Dad stands up from behind his desk. I hold my breath as he walks toward me, then holds my arms. "Exhibit patience, for starters. I know you love this place and want it to do well. You don't have to prove anything."

I step out of his circle of power. "Another way to say you don't believe I can."

His tone flips like a switch. "Don't come in here and try to browbeat me, kiddo. It ain't gonna happen."

I fix him with what I think is a disarming smile but I'm sure comes off more like I'm constipated. "I wasn't raised to back down," I answer with a lift of my chin. I know I sound like a tired war movie, but it's his language, so I speak it. Dad dismisses me by pointing at the door.

Dom's kneeling by my chute, straightening the parachute lines, when I stomp over.

"Whoa!" he says, grabbing my hand. "Spill."

"Commander Crotchety in there"—I thumb toward the office—"refuses to let me be part of the big-way we're doing to lure the X Games here." Dom's eyes go wide. I've lit up his entire brain with visions of glory. "He says I need to be perfect, *precise*. I can land my pinky toe on a penny in the middle of the DZ. I've done tons of formation jumps with you guys. What else do I have to do to show him?"

He holds my jumpsuit out for me to step into. "You know that famous thing where Babe Ruth points to the outfield and calls it?"

"Not really, but what's your point?" I ask, punching my arms into the suit.

"Call it." When I show no sign of understanding, he zips me up and adds, "Call your opening altitude and call where you'll touch down. Be precise about it. Hotdog your descent and stick the landing. Make it pretty. I'll film it so you can show him how good you are. He's too busy to watch you, so he doesn't see that you're a badass skydiver."

"He doesn't see me, period."

I look away from Dom's sympathetic eyes. Already a radical plan is formulating. The most radical I've ever had. Maybe you don't have to die to earn Dad's respect. Maybe you just have to show him you're not afraid to. "Pack it to open fast," I tell Dom.

"Boldly go." He smirks.

"You bet your ass. Where no *man* has gone before."

He gets back to folding my chute. Then he looks up at me. "And babe, I'm putting a penny in the dirt."

I rip a page from the back of someone's jump log and write on it, then march it into Dad's office. He doesn't even look at me or the paper as I toss it on his desk and about-face, slinging my helmet over my shoulder.

———

The pilot goes full throttle for takeoff, engines thunder, and the plane vibrates with power. Cold air sneaks in under the jump door next to me as I mentally run through what I'm about to do. We rumble down the runway, and I try to ignore the eyes of the other jumpers on me; recalling the eyes in the mirror causes unfamiliar nerves to fire off in my belly. I don't know if it's the memory of ghostly eyes in the motor home or what I'm about to do, but I've never been this on edge before a jump. My stomach is a taut, jelly-filled drum.

Once every other skydiver has exited the plane, I hold the metal edges of the doorway and lean forward into the wide open. Deep breath in, blow it out, and dive. Cool air hits my skin and presses like a giant hand against my torso. I go immediately into track position, hurtling through the pink-and-blue sky like a dart until I'm directly over the clean circle in the desert where I'm to execute a perfect landing. I ease into my arch.

There's nothing to do now but fall.

It's odd being out here alone again for the second time today, not part of a formation, and not goofing off with Dom, kissing in freefall. It's extremely lonely, like I'm disassociated from what I'm doing. Like maybe I'm not real. Not as if I'm dreaming. More like ... like I could be someone else's dream.

What if I was?

If I bounced, would another girl sit up in bed, sweating and panting, grateful it was just a dream?

This thought spooks me, makes me distrust myself for the first time, and this is one jump where I can't afford doubts. Every fluttering gnat of fear in my belly is squashed by the weight of my stubborn will. I have to do this. The risk I'm taking is worth it. It is. I'll show my father I'm precise.

The number I wrote on the slip of logbook said simply *1K*. I wish I could see his face when he realizes what it means — eight hundred feet below oh-shit altitude, where we must make a decision in an emergency. I had to turn off my automatic activation device to do this jump.

I'd laugh if the wind weren't pulling my cheeks back to my ears.

Dom is filming me, and I'm going to give him something memorable. But I can't fight the lonely drag as I fall; it's like no one, not even God, is watching me right now. I think of the specter eyes in the mirror, the spooky sensation of being watched instead of being the watcher. How can my own reflection scare me so much?

For a moment in that motor home, I was my own ghost.

I blow through the altitude where I'd normally pull. But this is no normal jump. I've had one jump when my chute failed to open and I had to deploy a reserve. This time, this one time, if there is a problem, I won't have time to deploy my reserve. My objectives are: Pull as low as I can. Don't die.

It's like playing chicken with the earth.

With every five hundred feet I lose, my heart hammers five hundred beats faster. My fingers are twitching to pull. It's all I can do not to reach for the cord. The ground is rushing at me so fast, and I can see people lined up around the drop zone. I'm certain I'll hear their gasps on the video later.

There's no taking my eyes off my altimeter now. I reach one thousand feet above ground level and pull, and my chute fans open in a violent gust. My legs swing hard underneath me as the chute jerks me upright. I do a quick check of the canopy and lines as I grab the toggles, realizing I have time for one-quarter of my turn before my feet touch the earth. I slam into the ground and roll. All breath has been knocked from me. Desperately I struggle for oxygen, but my body refuses to take in air.

For too long, all I see is white.

Did I ever pull at all?

Did someone just cry out in her sleep?

Peripheral vision opens up, color streams in fragments,

and footsteps batter toward me. Dom stares down with the video camera pointed at my face. A wild-eyed mania has replaced his normally cool expression. I scared him. I excited him too, but the dilated fear is still in his eyes.

"Jesus, Ry! That was . . . Whooo! You are unbelievable!"

I fight to pull air into my lungs. Now the camera is annoying me. Avery skids up next to him. "What, are you crazy?"

"What, are you new?" my voice croaks. As I start to push myself up, my fingers alight on something smooth and hard in the dirt. I grab it and hold it out to the camera with a wide smile. "The penny, bitches."

Dom stops filming and holds his hand out to help me up. "Damn, that was something. When I said 'call it,' I didn't mean for you to call a suicide altitude. I don't know if I'd ever do that," he says, much more serious.

I glare at him and his backpedaling support. "Well, those who can't do . . . dare."

"I didn't dare you to do *that*."

I gather my chute, and when I look up, I notice my father leaning against the golf cart, his arms folded and face deep red, mouth set into a grim line. Instead of looking impressed, he looks . . . murderous.

FOUR

"YOU WANT TO tell me what the hell you thought you were doing?" my father demands like a carnival barker in front of everyone who's gathered around.

I thrust my chin up. "I was being *precise*."

He shoves off the cart and is in my face immediately. "You're lucky you're not precisely dead! One problem, goddamn it! That's all it would have taken. One! And you'd be in the ground, DOA!"

"I wanted to show—"

"All you did, young lady, was prove to me how reckless and irresponsible you are!"

I fling my chute on the ground between us. "I showed I have the skill!"

"Bullshit. You showed you don't belong on my DZ. I don't need the job of shoveling your foolish ass off the dirt."

"Girl's got balls, man!" someone yells out.

"More balls than you," I say through clenched teeth. I know it's a low blow. "You're a coward, Dad. You're too scared to give me a chance to prove myself. I'm invisible to you. What in the hell do I have to do?" I shove him in the chest, and even I'm surprised at the rage I feel toward him. The detached observer in me wonders if it's the adrenaline.

Dad steps back, catching himself from falling. He rakes his hands over his buzzed hair like he's got to do something with his hands in order not to strangle me. His voice switches to a low growl, which is scarier than his barking lecture. "Get off this airport right now." He throws himself into the golf cart and peels out, spitting dust at me in its wake.

Dom and I walk back to the hangar in silence. I'm numb; I don't even flinch when a snake slithers out of the sagebrush in front of us, crosses our path, and slips into the dry weeds. He puts his arm around my shoulder and stops me. "You gotta understand, your dad, he—"

"Don't tell *me* about my dad!" I yell, shrugging out from under his arm. "Piss off."

"Don't be a bitch to me. I didn't make you do it, Ry. You managed to fuck up all on your own."

"Oh my God! Hop aboard the Ryan-will-slap-you express!" I shove him, too. Not once, but twice, hard in his chest. His black hair covers one eye. The other narrows with anger. Whatever. If people don't want to be attacked, why do they rattle my cage?

Mom is standing in front of the hangar as I walk up. Dad's hastily parked golf cart bakes in the sun next to her. She wrings her hands, waiting for me to approach. Her face doesn't look reprimanding; it's sad.

"You're not going to lecture me too, are you?"

"Go home, poppet. Check on your grandmother. I'll speak to you later. In the meantime, why don't you ponder the treasure that is this life, 'cause, baby girl, you spend it like it's cash burning a hole in your pocket."

On a normal day our house is cornea-stabbing white, but after I cry in the car for ten minutes as I drive home, it's like staring into the face of the sun. I squint as I walk toward it: a study in straight lines and right angles. Modern rectangular boxes of gleaming stucco contrast with black beams and walls of glass. Mom often hoses off the sides of the house, trying to beat back the desert that surrounds us. I think she's afraid she'll wake up one day and everything in her world will have turned to beige.

We've managed to create an oasis out of the three things that tolerate the heat of the Mojave Desert: palm trees, a flowering shrub called pride of Barbados (Mom loves that), and cacti.

Cacti are creepy. Joe and I joke that they are aliens waiting for a command from the mother ship. If this happens, my family is toast. We're completely surrounded.

I admit a few are strangely beautiful, with improbable flowers that seep out of them like colorful dew. But most are otherworldly petri-dish experiments magnified by a million. Some are tall and arty, while others look like pissed-off cucumbers.

Mom is obsessed with these beautiful, strange, and prickly creatures. Maybe that's why she's attracted to my father. She doesn't say it, but I think she resents that we have to live in this barren wasteland because Dad can't take the high stimulus of cities and people.

The thought of him and our fight makes me feel like my heart tripped and fell on a cactus.

The sound of Gran's piano welcomes me on the steps. I walk in, quiet enough not to distract her but loud enough not to startle. She's bent reverently over the keys. Her eyes are closed, hiding the clouds of her blindness. She's intent, her head cocked to the side like she's listening to someone else play. Her fingers are the most youthful thing about her, still nimble and straight, and I wonder if the rest of her body would be if she used it as much as she does her hands.

The music is a strange, mesmeric tune I've never heard before. "What is that you're playing?" I ask, gently placing my car keys on the glass kitchen table and walking over.

"My song. I want to give you my song."

My grandmother can be all kinds of perplexing sometimes. "Your song?"

"Of course," she says, not bothering to mask her impatience. Gran's moods have become pretty unpredictable as her dementia amps up. "Every person has a secret song only they can hear," she explains, digging deeper into the keys so that I hear the light tap of her too-long nails on the ivory. I'll need to cut them for her soon. "I'm playing my soul's song. Mine alone. But if I don't share it with you, then when I die, it'll die with me."

I sit down on the bench next to her warm body and hope that blind people can't smell tears. "Why does it have to die with you?" I ask softly.

"Because you are a stubborn cur who won't learn to play the piano."

I smile. "Mean old lady."

She starts her song over. I have to admit, it sounds like *her*. This is the only time I've ever felt bad for having no inclination to play. "Can it be sung?" I ask, wanting her to know I'd keep her song alive if I could, even if I had to hum it.

"No. You don't get to say how it comes through," she scolds. "You get your song the way you get it," she adds in that *you'll eat it and like it* tone, as if we're talking roast chicken.

No song has ever come through for me. "Maybe not everyone gets a song, Gran. I don't have one."

"Nonsense. You aren't listening, child. The blazing wildfire can't hear the soft wings of birds. Quiet yourself and you'll hear it. I warn you, don't die without sharing your song."

Gran and her voodoo warnings.

I don't like this topic. It strums the spooked chords I've already felt vibrate twice today. I glance behind me, daring myself to scan the long, straight shadows of the house. A quiver starts at my feet and hands and rises up my body. I wonder if a person freezing to death or dying does so from the outside in, like an ice cube. Is the middle—the house of your heart—the last to freeze? I shake my head to clear the random, strange thought. What the hell's the matter with me?

I concentrate on the piano and its lilting music. My eyes slowly find focus, and then I see a rippling movement within the polished veneer of the piano. Looking harder, I could swear the whites of eyes stare at me from the shiny black surface. I spin around again to check if someone's behind me. When I turn back, the eyes are gone.

Gran stops playing abruptly. She cocks her head and says, "Oh! Who have you brought home with you?"

The shiver reaches my neck and lies there like a cold hand. "No one, Gran. I'm alone."

Gran and her talk of death has made me edgier than I already was. I take her hand, grateful for its warmth. "C'mon, time for your bath."

It's not that my grandma needs everything done for her, but she's a little rickety lately. The first time I had to help her bathe, I apologized all over myself. "Nonsense." She laughed. "I had to pick boogers out of your nose and wipe the filth out of your little brown biscuits. This is payback."

Bath time has become our new normal. I love the waves of her hair when it's wet and I scrub her scalp gently with the pads of my fingers. I'm less shocked by the glimpse into my body's future than I was the first time I saw her naked. She can't see my eyes on her, and I try not to take advantage of that, but still I look. I make myself do it because I can't stand to let a mongrel like fear back me down. I'm not afraid of much, but I am afraid of getting old. I fear my back crooking like a bent finger. I fear clouds covering my sight.

I fear my mind will start to slip in puddles of thoughts like hers does.

I fear I'm seeing things.

After I'm done with her hair, Grandma washes her girl bits, and then I help her out of the tub to dry off, wrapping a huge white towel over her skin. She reminds me of an over-ripe banana: soft, brown, and spotted. Grandma shrugs me off and says, "Go on. That'll be Joe on the phone."

"The phone hasn't rung, Gran—" Phone rings. Of course it does. "Witchy! You creep me out when you do that!"

"Embrace the mysteries of life, child. I skipped ahead in time and came back to tell you."

I run to pick up the phone and smile through my hello when I hear Joe's voice.

"I have to come hang with you tonight. I've caught wind that among this evening's dinner guests, my mom has invited the son of a coworker as a potential blind date."

"Why don't you want to meet him?"

"He's too clean-cut," Joe answers. "Looks like a banker."

"So? You're all prep on the outside."

"Yeah, but I'm all freak underneath."

I laugh. Joe always makes me laugh. And he's right. He's Polo over pierced nipples. "Okay, JoeLo, come on over. I'll protect you from the scary gay banker."

I hang up and go to my room. I'm thrashed, bonking—probably adrenaline from the jump. I crawl atop my bed, flop back against the heaps of pillows, and stare at the galaxy of twinkle lights that reflect off the strings of small round mirrors hanging above me like stars. Undulating circles shimmer on the ceiling and the walls. My room of stars is the only place I can relax.

Usually I would turn on some music, but this time I don't. I lie on the bed and listen to the silence ringing in my ears and try really hard to hear my song, wondering what will happen if I die without hearing it.

FIVE

"WAKE UP, SUNSHINE. You're supposed to be my party to-night."

I'm bouncing. Why am I bouncing? My eyes flutter open to see Joe's face and his multitone, spiky hair. "For someone so paranoid about cacti overtaking the world, I wonder why you make your hair look like one."

Joe is hovering inches above me, staring down with his gap-toothed grin. Except for the twinkle lights, the room is dim with blue dusk. I clamp my hands on Joe's cheeks and slowly pull his face to mine, reveling in the terrified look in his eyes right before I bite his bottom lip hard. Laughing, I roll out from under him.

"Ow! Rawr," he says, with his fingers on his lips.

"I made you nervous. Don't lie," I say, still giggling.

Joe sits pretzel-style on my bed. "Noooo." His face admits defeat. "Okay, yes. You have just enough man energy about you to tempt me."

"That's because I'm in touch with my masculine side." I cross my legs opposite him, knee to knee, like we used to do when we were in our "summoning the spirits" phase of life. "Was your mom mad at you for ditching her dinner party?"

"Marginally. It's a five Hershey's Kisses infraction."

"You should own stock. I wish I could buy my parents off with chocolate. Do they sell Kisses the size of a Buick?"

"What'd you do now?"

I wave him off. "Why don't you want to at least meet the guy?"

"Because I'm pretty certain that my mother's taste in men is not my taste in men. Exhibit A: my dad."

"Most gay kids are worried their parents won't even accept them being gay, and she's trying to hook you up? That's pretty cool. It could be way worse."

He throws up his hands. "Yeah, well there are different kinds of narrow-mindedness. She's been psycho lately. She even signed me up for a Jewish LGBT mixer. My mom wants me to go because, as she puts it, 'I don't care if you date boys. But you'd better date a nice *Jewish* boy.'"

My phone buzzes next to the bed. A picture of Dom

pops up. I ignore it. I also try to ignore Joe's raised eyebrow. "Blowing off his call? Might I hope that you and Testosterone Tom—"

"Dom."

"Whatever. Are you fighting?" he asks with too hopeful a tone.

"Don't be a Dom-o-phobe. He just pissed me off earlier."

Joe's not one for evasions or half stories. His blue eyes fix me with that look that means I have to tell him the story of my big crap-ass day. Except for the part about wigging out in the motor home. How can I explain that someone else's haunted eyes were looking into mine from the mirror? Bumps erupt on my arms, because just thinking of the eyes makes me feel like they're watching me now.

After I tell Joe about my dad, the business failing, my risky jump, and the subsequent fight, Joe picks at his nails with a grave expression.

"What?"

"I don't get the things you do sometimes. When we were younger, you were my hero. It was you who showed me how to be unapologetically me. Full disclosure—I totally thought you were nuts, but your bravery made me want to be more brave. You're the reason I had the guts to come out. I wanted to live as out loud as you did."

"Thanks?" My jaw clenches.

"You used to thrill me, Ryan. Now ... now you scare me."

I swallow hard. "Stop being overdramatic. So I did something risky. Everyone takes risks now and then, especially when they want something."

"Your idea of risk is very different from most people's. Why do you have to up the ante all the time? I'd hate for you to find out the hard way that there's a limit."

Do I have an answer to this? I'm not sure I've ever thought about it. "I *need* extra stimulus, Joe—"

"There's a joke in there."

I ignore that. "I need it or I feel numb. Like there's an on/off switch in me, and adrenaline flips that switch. It's how I was made. How can that be wrong? You say I scare you, and the truth is, I *like* your fear. It tells me I'm different from the rest. *Special.*" That last word falls as a whisper.

Joe twirls his finger in the air around his ear. "Maybe *crazy* is another word for *special.*"

"*Crazy* is something flatliners call people like me," I say. "It makes them feel better about being boring."

"I'll ignore the fact that you just insinuated that I'm a boring flatliner. So, it's not about getting attention?"

Ouch. The way he asks this, I know he thinks it is. I crawl

into his chest. Through his T-shirt, his nipple ring pushes against my cheek as his arms wrap around me. It's easier to talk real when I don't have to look in his eyes. "Sometimes, with my dad especially, I feel invisible. I think the worst thing in life is to be invisible," I admit.

He doesn't give an answer just to give one. And he never judges. I love that about him. It's how he gets me to confess things to him I'd hardly admit to myself.

I sigh. "When you knock and no one seems to hear, you knock louder."

Joe starts to touch my hair and then stops himself like a good and proper best friend. My hair does not like being touched. "Honey, you could never be invisible. Not you. You're trumpets and neon and hot sauce."

"You say the sweetest things," I tell him, rolling up to primp in the mirror, trying to smooth down my wild mane of ringlets. Dizziness overtakes me as if I've stood too quickly. I grasp the edge of my dresser, bow my head, and take a deep breath until it passes. Once it does, I inhale at my image in the mirror. A ghostly hand appears to be touching my hair. I look down at my own hands, still clenched on the wood in front of me.

When I look up again, the hazy outline of a face presses forward at me like ice rising from the bottom of a glass.

Spectral eyes bore into mine, staring with the curious but grim expression of someone watching a nature show, knowing they're going to see the death of the brave animal whose panicked run for its life is about to end.

Six

Joe regards me with narrowed eyes and his head cocked to one side. It's me he's watching, not the mirror. Why? Because he can't see what I'm seeing. I'm seeing things that aren't there, right?

"I'm buggin' in this room." My voice is breathy, struggling to restrain a scream. "I need to get out of here. Let's go to the hill."

Mom doesn't bat an eye when she sees me grab some cranberry juice from the fridge. It'll go good with the vodka I have stashed in my bag.

"Ah, ah, ah," she says as I try to slip out the front door with Joe. "Not so speedy, young lady. What you did today," she says, raising herself from her favorite chair, "was dangerous and reckless. You mustn't cause undue stress for your father. You know the concerns on his shoulders. You know what he struggles with."

Eyes say more than words do. For most of my childhood, Mom's eyes were weighted with worry. The pinched look faded for a while, but it's back with a vengeance. She's worried that he'll start being explosive again, or worse, retreat from us into that dark inner place — the shadowy cave of his heart — and that there might come a time when he'll crawl so far in we can't reach him. The way her eyes narrow at me, I think she's worried I'll be the one to push him over his edge.

Funny how she forgets that my father's not the only one with shadows inside.

At the crest of the hill is a narrow dirt road where Joe parks his car and cuts the engine. California City — "the Land of the Sun," as the sign aptly proclaims — glimmers below us to our left. Every other direction is dark but for the string of headlights snaking north and south on Highway 395.

The hill can't be called a secret place. Too many desert people crave a scenic overlook, and this scrubby dot is the only one for miles. Luckily, it's rare for anyone to be up here on a weeknight. When you have the hill all to yourself, it feels like you own the world. Harsh, flat wilderness stretches out in every direction. Out here, I'm the center of a compass. When a strong gust of wind kicks up, I feel like I can be lifted off the hill and blown anywhere. I like the randomness of that. The adventure.

I gulp some juice out of the plastic bottle to make room for vodka, add the booze, then replace the cap and give it a good shake. All the while, Joe watches me, chewing on his thick thumb. "You have sausage fingers." I hold the bottle out to him. "Want some?"

He shakes his head. "Driving."

"Good answer. One of us has to be the mature one." My tone's a bit more sardonic than I meant it to come out.

"Want to tell me what ghost passed through you back in your room?"

My eyes snap up to meet his. Joe has no idea how interesting his choice of words is. I *feel* like I met a ghost.

"Huh. I was hoping I played that off."

"Please, I know you better than that. You've been my best friend since first grade."

I smile. Our story will go down in history as the friendship that started because a little boy came to school on Halloween as Dorothy from *The Wizard of Oz* and a little girl kicked some bully booty that day. Ironically, I was dressed as Batman, but you didn't see anyone jeering at me the way they did at Joe. Even then, the hypocrisy was not lost on me. "You rocked those sparkle shoes."

"You were saying . . ."

Clear throat. Decide whether to tell the truth. Decide that I can't *not* tell him. "You have to promise to keep it to yourself."

"Does *that* even need to be said?"

"No." The spiked juice goes down easy, and I gulp some more, hoping the warmth will chase the damp chill of dread out of my bones. I tug my picnic blanket from my bag and get out of the car, wrapping it around my shoulders as I sit on the warm hood. The light wind makes the edges of the blanket flap like the sound of a parachute. I close my eyes and imagine being up there right now, floating in the stars. What would it feel like to fall up?

The car door shuts loudly when Joe gets out, snapping me back to the moment. We both know I'm stalling. I look at my lap as I speak. Bite my lip. Stop myself from curling into a ball. "I think I'm losing it."

"That would imply you hadn't already, my love."

I sock him in the leg. "Three times today, I could swear I saw someone looking back at me out of my reflection."

"Ryan, isn't that, like, the very definition of *reflection*?"

"Someone besides me, dope!"

His smile says, *C'mon, quit screwing around,* but it fades

when he sees how serious I am. "I—I don't know what to do with that information."

"Me neither."

"It's not normal to see other people when you look in the mirror."

"You don't say."

Lights bounce erratically behind us, and we both realize that someone is coming up the hill. Dom rumbles up next to us in his brother's car. He smiles at me, no trace that we had a fight earlier.

"Hey."

"Hey."

Dom chin-lifts to Joe. "What's up, man?"

"Oh, ya know, gas prices, value of Apple shares, concerns over America's increasing military presence in foreign countries . . ." I nudge Joe in the ribs, and he hops off the hood. "I'd better be getting back. I'm guessing you might want to stay?" he asks me with his hands stuffed in his pockets. I still don't get why Joe doesn't like Dom. If he would only get to know him . . . Seems Joe's nonjudgmental ways stop at Dom's door.

"I'll stay." I slide onto my feet and kiss Joe's cheek. "Call you tomorrow. Love you."

We watch him back up and pull away. His engine fades as it descends the hill.

"C'mere," Dom says, holding out his arms.

My hands are on my hips as I take one soldier step toward him and halt. Dom bows his head and rubs his jaw, trying to hide his smile behind his hand. He takes one step toward me, stops.

Crickets chirp in the night around us.

"Still mad?" His voice is soft.

I take another step forward. "Not really."

His move. "I'm sorry."

One step. "Me too."

We are one last footstep away from each other, both of us smiling. Dom draws a line in the sand between us with the toe of his boot.

"Daring *me* to cross the line?" I ask with a laugh. "That's like asking a tiger not to eat meat!"

"Ha! After today, *tiger*, I know there's no line you won't cross if you really want to." He bites his bottom lip in that slow way that invites attack, and fixes me with sultry cinnamon eyes. "Want to?"

Trusting him to catch me, I pounce, wrapping my legs around his waist as he holds me up. His jeans scratch pleasantly against my bare calves. When I grab both sides of his head and kiss him hard, hungry, he matches my force with lips seasoned with a bit of guy sweat and cool mint. I tease them open with my tongue, exploring, tasting. He's my cake.

The moon is a spotlight on Dom's upturned face, bathing him in an incandescent blue glow. I trace the light on his heart-shaped lips with my fingers. It's such a turn-on the way his breathing intensifies and his mouth opens when he wants me.

I yank his T-shirt sideways to expose his corded neck and shoulder and revel in his groan when I bite the tattoo there. A sense of power rolls over me when I leave a mark. It's exhilarating to pull my shirt over my head and throw it on the ground. The desert blows on my skin like it's making a wish, and I think that we, clutching each other on this mountain, are the pin the world revolves around.

Dom's gaze devours my bare skin.

I am black silk against the moon.

He lifts me higher to clamp his mouth on me, and I cradle his head against my chest; my face burrows into his black hair. It tickles my neck. He carries me to the car and sets me down softly on the hood, my bare back registering the residual warmth of the engine's heat. But the warmth that radiates through me has nothing to do with the car. My fingers rip open his jeans, and I push him away with my foot to squirm out of my shorts. He moves my foot off his belly and runs his hands down my thighs. The question burns in his eyes.

My answer is to hook my heels around his back and pull him to me.

"I don't have a condom," he whispers, pressing his body against mine.

"I want you now, Dom."

I love that first push.

All of them, really.

I like how we say no more words but have expressed . . . everything.

"Do you see that?" I point to the east. Miles away, flashes of lightning split the sky, flickering across it in enormous white sheets. It's so far away I can't hear the thunder. There's hot wind, though, and it whips against my skin as I stand naked on the hilltop with my arms stretched over my head. I feel feral. Elemental, like lightning could shoot from my fingertips.

Clicking noises fire off behind me. "Put that camera down," I tell Dom. "Can't you enjoy the moment without filming or snapping pictures?" I don't actually mind, though. He sees something through that lens that magnifies reality.

"Nope. I have to capture you in all your wild glory. You

don't know how ragingly beautiful you are. You're larger than life, Ry."

I look over my shoulder and think, *If I were, would I have to prove it all the time?*

A rueful smile passes over my face. That sounds like something Joe would ask me. Or my dad. Why is brave only brave if it's saving a life or fighting for your country? Why isn't it considered brave to live your life to the fullest? I see so many people afraid to do that simple thing. We all die. Might as well skid into death, breathless and laughing, with life still clinging to you like perfume.

My clothes are scattered on the desert floor, so I gather them up and give them a shake, in case a spider or scorpion has scrabbled inside, before slipping them back on. Dom stares at the faraway lightning with his brows furrowed. He's got some words for me—probably about our fight today—and is trying to figure out how to spit them out.

"I have to tell you something," he finally says, which makes my hands curl into fists. "Your dad asked me to be in charge of the big-way for the corporate suits."

"Great!" Maybe there's hope after all. "So you can add me—"

"He's given me firm orders that you are not to be included in the jump." I spin around to face him. His forehead creases as though he's cringing to tell me this. "I know how bad you want to do it. I'm sorry, babe."

"I *will* do it."

"I gave my word."

His voice rings with apology and helplessness, but that's not soothing me. "You promised to screw me out of helping my family? Out of possibly being a part of the X Games? What about being fair to me? You know my dad's being unreasonable."

"It's not my call. If it were, I'd let you do it."

"You're not one of his soldiers. Not every one of his orders has to be followed."

"This one does. I hate to put it this way, but it's not about you, so don't pull any crap and jeopardize this for the rest of us or jeopardize your family's business. It's too important."

While Dom has remained calm, my feelings are a tempest in the middle of my chest. I stand in the summer wind and puff through my nose like a bull deciding whether or not to charge. I want to light into him, even though it's not his fault. I want to rip the goddamn wings off my dad's planes. I want the entire big-way team to throw their rigs on the ground and refuse to jump unless I'm with them, like some movie football team. I want my dad to shake his head in defeat and say yes, yes, of course I'm needed.

Yes, I'm good enough.

Yes, I'm worthy.

One thing I won't do is cry the tears that are closing up my throat and blurring my eyes. Behind all this talk of being "special" and "larger than life," I realize, I just want a normal little thing, my father's love and respect, and I'm sure he's not capable of giving it to me.

"Say something." Dom reaches for me. "It's scary when you're quiet like this. I don't know if you're calming down or plotting to bend the world to your will."

I'm sure as hell not going to bend to the world's will.

This defiant declaration is poised on my tongue, but I don't say it. Instead I fall into the arms of the person who gets me because he's so much like me. While Dom may be a calmer version, we both have unpredictable storms inside us. We both follow our hearts. We both get high off pushing the envelope. I admire that about us. If no one ever went outside of acceptable limits, we'd never know what we're capable of. I know I'm capable of doing this jump, of helping my family, of earning my dad's respect.

"I want to be part of something special."

"Look in the mirror, Ryan. *You* are something special."

The mirror...

"I don't want to look in any more mirrors today."

Remorse hits me. He probably thinks I'm talking about

his idea to play in front of the mirror. "I don't mean us," I try to explain, but I can't possibly explain *this*. Especially not when I'm attempting to convince him I can do the big-way.

My reflection is supposed to be mine alone. Now it's like someone else is trying to step out from it. I hope this day was a glitch in the wiring, some kind of temporary mental speed bump. There's the live-life-on-the-edge brand of crazy and the seeing-spirits-in-the-mirror brand of crazy.

I've felt more cold fear this day because of those searching, ghostly eyes than I did with pulling my chute at a thousand feet. That thrilled me but scared everyone else.

Better to be feared than fearful.

SEVEN

DOM PULLS THE car into my driveway, shuts the lights off, and turns toward me. "I've got something special you can be a part of," he says. "Mauricio's planning a party. You want to go on a little trip in the motor home?"

"My folks are never going to let me go off on a trip with you and your brother in some stranger's abandoned motor home. Where do you guys think you're going?"

"Nowhere . . . everywhere . . ."

I pinch his arm. "*No hablo* mysteriously vague."

"We're gonna do LSD."

"LSD? As in peace, love, and sixties? LSD as in dancing like a chicken in a blender with your top off in the rain? That stuff's still around?"

"I know! It's old-school cool. Mauricio's done it a few times, says it's the ultimate mind trip, totally expanding.

He said he never experienced anything like it." Dom lifts his camera and snaps a shot of the frog-legged underside of a giant June bug on the windshield. "We're having a small, private party tomorrow night in the motor home. It won't leave the hangar. We figured it'll be a safe, isolated place. Contained — in case anyone wigs out."

"Wigs out?"

His face lights up like an explorer. "I've always wanted to try it, to see for myself how mind-expanding it is. It could be great for my art. Feel like doing it with me? It'd be another first for us."

My insides warm. Dom and I have had many firsts.

The porch light flicks on, and my father's silhouette fills the doorway. He points at the ground directly in front of him. I guess I'm supposed to run right over there and stand at attention like a good little soldier. Or his dog.

I clench my jaw, lean over to kiss Dom's cheek, and whisper, "What the hell. I'm in. You only live once."

My dad starts up before I've even reached him.

"Where have you been?" His eyebrows are so pinched I bet I could store a quarter in the grooves above his nose.

"You grounded me from jumping. I didn't realize you grounded me from life."

"I want to talk —"

I shove past him through the front door. "Oh, *now* you

want to talk to me? That's novel. You took jumping away from me, the one thing I love to do more than anything. Punishment has been meted out. Go back to your regularly scheduled programming and leave me alone."

"Don't give me your smart mouth, Ryan. Jumping isn't the only thing I can take away from you."

"In less than one month I'll be eighteen, and you won't have a say in what I do!"

He steps forward, gets all up in my face. "That's right. In one month you can move out, support yourself, screw up your own life, and be responsible for the fallout. But for now, your ass belongs to me, and you will obey me. Got it?"

"My ass belongs to no one!" I rage back. "You're so short-sighted, Dad. Take away skydiving—go ahead. I'll get my kicks some other way. It's my life!"

He jabs a finger toward my nose. "Don't threaten me, kid. I've dealt with worse punks than my own surly, stubborn daughter."

"Enough!" Mom yells. It's so rare to hear her raise her voice that it shocks both of us out of our trenches. Her face is a black storm, threatening rain. "What is it about the two of you that rattles each other so? You're like a couple of spitting roosters, dancing around with your chests puffed out. I don't like this fighting, this disharmony in my home. Stop it, now!"

"Hose 'em off like you do the house," Gran chimes in.

Dad throws up his hands and stalks away, leaving a vapor of anger behind him, but Mom is there to pick up where he left off. "You have a grand sense of timing, don't you? Can't you see that he's under tremendous pressure?" Her voice descends to a whisper. "I told you earlier, someone in his condition shouldn't be under such stress. Why are you adding to it?"

"By standing up for myself?"

"Uh, child of mine! At least call it what it is!"

"A tantrum!" Gran blurts. I wish she could see me roll my eyes at her.

Mom blows out an exasperated breath. "Lay low for a few days. I've got my hands full enough with your daddy and the business."

"But Mom, he —"

She turns her back and walks away, mumbling something about how she doesn't need to attend every fight she's invited to.

Gran shuffles across the room and straight to me like a homing beacon. "I used to have to rub your mama's legs when she was a girl, growing pains were so bad."

"Yeah?" I answer noncommittally. Who knows where Gran's going with this. It'll either be gibberish or a frying pan of hot truth upside the head.

"I suspect *your* growing pains will be the kind I can't rub out."

"Maybe," I answer. I know I sound obstinate. I'm so freaking exhausted all of a sudden.

Gran's broken eyes somehow bore into mine. It's unnerving. "When you gonna realize that every threat you make to your parents is really a threat against yourself?"

"I'm tired. Can I just go to bed and have a do-over tomorrow, Gran?"

"Wish it worked that way, sugar. My advice is, don't go doing things you wish you could undo."

EiGHT

I THOUGHT SLEEP WOULD quiet me, but I'm too restless. It's not a physical restlessness; sex and skydiving smoothed that edge. It's a mental itch. My head is my problem. It wants to replay everything that scared me today, everything that stripped the protective coating off my wires. It wants to open doors labeled *fear, vulnerability,* and *self-doubt.*

I don't open those doors.

Not for anyone. Or any*thing.*

Behind what psychological door is the mirage girl hiding?

As soon as the house slips into the quiet hum of night, I slip out the back door. Sneaking out drunk and alone is the potent dose of rebellion I need after the fight with my dad, the lecture from my mom, and Gran's vague warnings. They gang up on me and expect that I'll swallow their bitter medicine without a chaser. Ha. I take another swig of my spiked cranberry juice and march down the road, using the raised road reflectors like braille so I don't veer off into the brush and disappear forever.

The night stills me. The sky is a cap of blue-black with constellations as familiar as Gran's age spots. I'm lost in it until a reflector winks light at me and I realize a car is approaching from behind. The tires make a sticky-wet sound on the asphalt as the car slows. It crawls alongside me as I walk the dusty shoulder. It's not the leering face of the crusty old man that kicks my adrenaline into high gear and sends my heart rocketing. It's her face, rolling up and over, up and over in the chrome rims: a ghost on wheels with eyes that promise to follow me everywhere.

With my heart beating drums in my temples, I turn back and run straight home.

Even in the safety of my room, in the cocoon of my bed, my mind spins like the face in those tires. I lie there and realize . . . every barred door is wide open.

I grit my teeth against the feelings. This haunt is pissing me off.

"See this cowbell?" Mauricio holds up a large copper bell dangling from a thick leather braid and gives it a good shake. It clangs through the motor home so loud that my eyes squint. "If anyone walks out the door, put the bell around your neck. That way we can find your dumb ass if you're wandering around in the desert."

The motley assortment of people chuckle and shuffle nervously. I imagine it would be terrifying to be lost in the vast desert while trippin' on hallucinogenic drugs. The Mojave Desert will swallow you whole and spit your bleached skeleton in the sand.

I'm glad to be in the safety of a closed hangar, but I have to admit, coming back into this RV makes me feel like I've walked into a meat locker. Not warm and safe like a cocoon in the summer, where humidity hides under the felt leaves of the succulents. In here it's snow and sand: a cold and rough paste against my skin.

Nibbling on chips, trying not to dwell on how boxed in I feel, I blow out a deep breath and look for Joe. He sits in the driver's seat of the RV, reading a book, and occasionally looks up at me through his blond lashes. He jerks his head toward the door with a question on his raised eyebrows. I'm not leaving. He won't either. No matter what I say, he won't let me do this without him being some kind of "trip sitter."

Dad would kill me if he knew what I'm about to do. But hey, I warned him. Skydiving gives me the rush I need. It makes me special and unique in the regular world. Without jumping out of airplanes, I'm . . . average, and average isn't where I want to be on life's curve. I'd seriously rather be dead than the walking dead. Besides, this is where it started. I figure if I can come in here and face down my fear, it'll stop haunting me.

There is a small group of us trying LSD for the first time. Avery's face is more white than normal, and I wonder why she's here. It's one thing if you're trying to prove something to yourself, a non-thing if you're trying to prove something to everyone else. I avoid her greedy, attention-seeking eyes. Half the time I don't know what Avery wants. Our relationship has never been an easy one. The last time we fought, it devolved into petty insults, the kind sisters sling at each other. I told her she was a phony. She laughed and accused me of being a hypocrite. She said she saw through me — that I acted like a big hotshot as a cover-up for feeling really small. She said *I* was the phony. We didn't talk for a spell. Since then we've been peaceful, but I feel prickly as a cactus around her.

The faces of the people in the motor home are not unlike those of a group of first-time jumpers. Masks of excitement overlaid upon fear. Anxiety is exposed by fidgety fingers and increased rates of speech. It shows in the eyes, for sure: a little more rounded than normal, with hollowed pupils that look like newly dug holes.

I've become convinced that no one can truly hide their fear.

I pat my own fear on the head. *Down, boy.*

Mauricio hands each of us a tiny, colorful paper square. "The blotter paper goes under your tongue," Dom whispers. I tilt my head like *duh,* but I had no idea. I slip the square in my mouth, wondering if it will dissolve or what. Dom and I take seats at either end of the couch, facing each other, wiggling our bare toes together. He starts video recording on his phone. Joe sits with his book propped up to his nose and tries to pretend he's not watching me like a bug under glass. I wink and wait to feel abnormal.

Mauricio approaches with a bowl in his hands. It's full of small folded notepapers. I wonder if I'm supposed to put one in my mouth, but we're instructed to put them in a pocket. "Read it when you need something to think about," he says with a knowing smirk. "Sometimes it's good to have a distraction if you're wandering down a bad street in your brain."

"Wait, isn't LSD supposed to bliss me out?" I ask, stuffing the paper into my pocket.

"Depends." Mauricio moves on to the next person.

"That's not an answer. Depends on what?"

Joe leans forward and taps my temple. "Probably on where your head's at to begin with."

I don't reply, because I'm thinking my head hasn't been Sanity Street and I haven't confided that to anyone but Joe. I'm already up shit creek. I don't need to sink my raft by telling everyone that I'm seeing someone who isn't there.

We're all sitting around talking and clowning, trying to act normal but watching one another closely like there's a booby prize for who will be the first to act tweaked. People are tossing around theories about who might have owned this RV. It's a terrorist plot—millions of RVs stored all over America will roll out like a giant bus army and attack us. It was abandoned by a family whose kid was killed by a stranger when they went camping, so they just wanted to walk away from it and the awful memories it holds. Maybe it was owned by a stinking-rich family who just uses stuff, then discards it. Maybe they'll never come get it, and we can raffle it off in a contest . . .

This is a strange phase where we're posturing like we're mellow and lighthearted, yet trying to ignore the zingy bolt of nervous anticipation that's threading around our bodies. How long does this period go on? It's hard to tell. The laws of time are rewritten, and I feel like maybe clocks don't even apply to us right now.

My hand slides over the edge of the couch, and my fingers brush against the Bible I know is there. It's heavy when I slip it free, like God's words are weightier than mere mortals'. I suppose they must be. I let the crisp papers flit by, kicking up dust that wrinkles my nose, allowing the book to come to a place where it wants to be opened. It's always been one of my favorite things to do, let fate decide where to place its finger on a page.

JAMES 5:14–15: *Is anyone among you sick? Let him call for the elders of the church, and let them pray over him, anointing him with oil in the name of the Lord. And the prayer of faith will save the one who is sick, and the Lord will raise him up. And if he has committed sins, he will be forgiven.*

Well, that seems useless. I'm not sick. Unless my recent head hiccups can be called sick . . . I wonder what being "anointed with oil" entails. It sounds kind of sexy. Glancing up at Dom, I think I'd like to anoint *him* with some oil. My attention bounces back to the book.

Handwritten names are inscribed in precise script in the back of the Bible: Isaiah, John, Mary, Matthew. All biblical names, with birth dates and death dates next to them. The last name, Rachel, has a birth date just a couple of years before mine. She was only seventeen when she died. How sad. Why would they leave their family Bible in their abandoned RV? I quickly slip the Bible back in its place.

This strange family's history presses me down like a giant thumbprint.

A faint metallic taste coats my mouth, like I've stuck my tongue on the tip of a battery. I find myself wondering if the heart is our body's battery. If so, what powers the heart? And then, what powers what powers the heart? Suddenly my own beating heart is the only thing I'm aware of. It thrums in the delicate round tips of every finger. It swells like a miniature version of our hill in the middle of my palm, then dissolves back into my lifeline. It surges under the vulnerable spots in my neck. It pulses in my crotch.

I am an enormous beating heart. I am a battery.

One guy starts dancing in the kitchen of the motor home, stomping around like some kind of shaman. I think he's dancing to the beat of my body.

Or maybe . . . maybe he's heard his song.

It occurs to me that my trip may have started in earnest when I realize I've been staring at Dom for what seems like days. His black hair is rippling currents in an ebony sea. I hear waves crash on the beach of his forehead. His eyes are swirling, foamy tide pools. I want to reach in and pluck secrets from little marbled shells. He catches me watching, stops panning the room with his camera, and smiles wide like he's happy I can finally see the truth about him.

Avery sticks her fingers in the current of his black waves,

mesmerized by *my* ocean. I slap her hand, and she wanders away, smiling.

Someone is playing a ukulele. I'm pleasantly shocked that I can *taste* the sound. I lean back and let the flavors of the music roll around on my tongue for a while. Major chords are sweet like butterscotch. Minor chords taste like flat gray rocks. We once had a pregnant neighbor who sucked on pieces of terra cotta. What was she hungering for?

I don't know how long I've been here. The motor home is driving down a timeless road.

Time dilates like a giant pupil opening and closing the great eye of time watches our every move I don't know if I've skipped ahead like my grandmother does or if I'm behind some of the other people who look static they pushed pause can we rewind I feel like there's not enough air in here air soup I have to move to circulate the air swirl the colors of it with my fingers painting streaks of life thoughts coming in rhyme and it's about time my soul unwinds beautiful threads of me unravel and I am the colorful scarf God wraps around her braids.

Stillness.

It's like my brain is taking a deep breath, sucking me back into myself.

I think about how they say you can't die in a dream or you'll die for real. Clarity strikes like lightning: We never die. Never. I feel like the universe has whispered a secret. *The* secret. We are as eternal as the winds that flow like rivers. The winds may change shape, direction, momentum, but they always *are*. I am in on a huge secret. I want to run through this house on wheels and announce it to everyone: we literally *cannot* die. Oh my God. Nothing I do matters.

I think I always knew this. My dad has drilled this point home with his actions and even with his words. I don't matter.

I am safe from death because I cannot die.

I stand and spread my arms wide, announcing, "Nothing I do matters!" No one answers me, which kind of proves my point.

There is no death. Only change.

This realization is so expansive that it scares me, makes me feel small, insignificant. I'm a gnat in outer space. I wonder if listening to familiar music will ground me. I put my earbuds in but don't press play because I realize I don't want other people's music right now.

Fear perks its ears up. Its long tongue lolls out, panting at my feet.

My grandmother planted a seed, and I'm afraid I'll never

see it blossom. I want to hear *my* song. I wonder how old she was when she first heard hers. I'll bet she heard it in the womb. I can see the truth about Gran's brain. Why does *dementia* sound like *demented*? They've got it all wrong. They don't know that that part of her brain resides in another dimension. They should call it *dimentia*.

I warn you, don't die without sharing your song.

But we can't die, Gran. Of all people, how does she not know this? It suddenly becomes enormously important that I find a way to hear my song. I feel panicky, like I'm in peril of eternal soul agony if I am sucked into the winds before I hear my song from this life. Or share it. Why didn't I ask her what happens if I don't?

There's a pit of writhing snakes in my belly.

I need to think about something else.

I frantically pull out the folded paper from my jeans pocket. It's a quote from someone named Bill Hicks:

> *There is no such thing as death; life is only a dream*
> *and we're the imagination of ourselves.*

Such unbelievable syncing with my thoughts that I know it's not an accident I got this slip of paper out of all the scraps. The universe is whispering again. I reread the quote. I'm already imagining things when I'm *not* on drugs.

If I'm the imagination of myself, then that means there are always two of me.

Is it this *other* me who follows?

Restless wandering, passing everyone in the kitchen and living room. I step over two girls reverently touching each other's faces as I head down the motor home's thin hallway. I look in the mirror, trying to summon her, this other me, to boldly face her down. I see myself. My lips are beautiful, pillowy and curved upward at the corners, like my mother's. I admire the strong structure of my collarbone and shoulders. I can see my heartbeat, a tantalizing pulsing pearl in the indent at my throat. I step closer, peer deep into myself. My eyes are so big and so black and I think . . .

That's the hole she crawls out of.

Suddenly she's there. We stare at each other, this girl and I. She watches me like I'm a rare species in a cage. And I watch her. I wonder whose vision is truer. Maybe her world is as real as mine. Maybe I *am* someone else's dream. Maybe she's as scared of me as I am of her. Wouldn't that be weird — we two, feeding each other's writhing snake?

Wind rushes through the motor home like a jump door's been opened. I slam on the glass with my fist.

Her eyes blink a delayed beat later.

A sharp chill seeps in through my listening ears, invades my breathless mouth, stabs my witnessing eyes. Every velvet inch of my black skin itches from the biting cold burrowing into my pores, and I fear that if I look down, I'll have turned white. Iced over.

She presses her palm to the mirror where mine rests and leans her forehead against the glass.

I suck in my breath and lean my head forward too. It's cold. So cold. But I do it because I feel seen, because I want to feel connected with someone, anyone. She knows I'm here. She invites me in. Reaches through the door and grabs me by the throat.

I lean into her, my mouth on the freezing window of her world, and think, *How strange . . .*

I feel

myself

freefall.

NINE

BSBD — BLUE SKIES, BLACK DEATH. That's what we say when a skydiver dies. But there's no blue sky around me, only bleak and utter darkness.

This freefall has me kicking wildly, my arms spinning and flailing, like I'm swimming, using every ounce of strength not to drown. She is wrapped around my torso, her weight an anchor. I'm struggling to keep her from pulling me under.

Soaking black yearning, hot red fury, and crystalline shards of glass. My whole world is distilled into color and feeling. This new, shiny blade of fear pierces me in the gut, cuts deeper than any feeling I've ever had.

I'm fighting for my life.

I punch at her, my fist meeting more glass. It shatters against my knuckles. Her grasp tightens. I kick harder, but my legs sink into blackness like thick mud. A scream rips from my throat. My voice cuts like diamonds. I taste the blood that runs down the back side of my tongue.

You're so cavalier, she tells me, her voice angry, accusatory, *to dance on the blade of life and death. And you're wrong . . . stupidly wrong. What you do* does *matter. Death is the end. You can die. You. Will. Die.*

Sharp shards of glass cut through me as I try to deny her words. She whispers that I've slipped from the knife's edge.

We tumble in the fall, and now I'm the one dangling, hanging on to *her . . .* on to myself . . . I look up at my body, at my own terrified beauty. I was a beautiful light. *Was.* One by one, my fingers rip away.

I drop from myself.

I am the leaf, drained of color, crumbling, quaking, as it falls from the tree.

TEN

THERE'S HEAVINESS IN coming out of freefall. Gravity has such strong hands. The body is constricting, a corset that's too tight. It's hard to take a full breath. The *beep-beep-beep* of a machine assaults me as the world of color and smells and sharp, stinging pain wrap around me like a barbed-wire blanket.

All senses are go.

A baby cries somewhere, and I intimately know how it feels, thrust into the wide open where anything can happen. It's confusing and scary. My body hurts. I feel like death, toasted on both sides.

It's hard to open my eyes, but I fight to, and realize I'm in the hospital. My tongue bursts with pinpricks. When I swallow, it's like nails raking down my throat. I attempt to push my voice up through the fire. "What happened?" Pain causes a hot tear to slide from the corner of my eye.

Someone's in the room, but they don't seem to have heard my raspy question. I try to move, but my body is concrete buried in gripping mud. Someone—Joe?—notices me struggling and rushes over, wraps his arms around me. I wince but let myself be held because it feels good: physical, warm, and reassuring.

"Oh my God, honey, you're finally awake. You wigged out on the acid is what happened," he says against my ear. His prickly hair stings my face.

Acid? Oh, of course.

"I tried to tell you not to do it. We talked about this. Really, how high do you think you can raise your stakes before you lose?"

I point to my raw throat, noticing my heavily bandaged arms and hands as I do. "Why—"

"You crashed right through the mirror like you were diving out of a plane."

I blink hard, trying to recall. The memory hides behind a gauzy veil. I can see the outline of it but not the full picture. "I walked *through* the mirror?" I choke out. Every word cuts.

"Yeah, that was bad enough, but then you flipped, went completely berserk, flailing and struggling like you were fighting off an attacker. I could barely get you under control, and then you went unconscious. There was blood everywhere." His kiss on my forehead is fragile. "I love you, you stupid, stupid—"

"You ever scare us like that again, and I'll kill you myself." That's my father's voice coming from the doorway. Chills roll over my body. He doesn't need to throw threats at me right now. I'm shaken enough. A father should be kissing my head and telling me he loves me. We stare at each other, and I suddenly remember: He's locked inside himself. Numb. He can't show me love.

Then my mother is against my side with tears in her eyes. She slips her palm gingerly beneath mine, trying to be careful of the cuts. "You lost a lot of blood. They couldn't stabilize your blood pressure. It was touch-and-go for a while." My stomach jerks. Can we stop talking about blood? I'm appalled with myself.

My mom is pale, her lips bare without bright color, like a bruised rose. I've frightened her, and shame warms its hands over the fire of guilt in my heart. "I'm happy you're all right," she says, "but I'm so disappointed in you. So very disappointed and astonished. How could you be this reckless with your life?"

"I'm . . . I'm not."

She rolls her eyes. "Baby, what do you think you've got if you don't have *life*?"

"Nothing. Emptiness." *It's nothing but darkness.* My voice is scratchy and flat, not my own. I feel like I need to break it in, but it hurts so much to speak. It's easier to let them all talk at me.

My mother's clenched fingers fly up to her mouth to hold in her sob. "You would take my only daughter from me!" She turns her back. Her words are a knife in my heart, and even now I appreciate the acute pierce of it, the evidence that I'm alive.

My grandmother shuffles over. Her tapered, wrinkled fingers hover over my skin as if she's feeling something beyond the borders of my body. Maybe her hands see what her eyes can't. Her hand suddenly pulls back to the breast of her flowered dress. She doesn't say anything, just shakes her head side to side like there are no words. Side to side: a metronome of sadness.

I don't feel like their child. Like anybody's child. I feel like the ax that's been slung through their lives. I guess I didn't think at all. I simply acted. And now I have to deal with the consequences. People want to be angry or sad, and despite how bad I feel, the strongest emotion I have right now is gratitude. Gratitude just to be alive.

"Forgive me."

ELEVEN

TWO DAYS LATER, I shield my eyes as I'm helped from the car to the house. My body feels alien as I move, but the more I do it, the more I sink into my skin. Being mummified in bandages from the numerous cuts isn't helping to make me feel normal. I'm glad it's summer and I don't have to face all the scrutinizing eyes at school. I need time. I'll have a lot of scars to remind me of that night. The only wound I cringe at is the one buried under gauze on my left cheek, which runs from my cheekbone to my chin. I will never look like me again.

"Thanks, Ayida," I say to my mother as she situates me on the gray couch, bolstering velvet poppy pillows around me and handing me a glass of lemonade. She darts a look my way at my use of her proper name, but I can't help it.

Everything is suddenly changed. You don't come back from where I've been unchanged.

I'm a different person now.

I look around, seeing home with new eyes. There is so much glass and luster that my reflection shines from nearly every surface. I can't help but stare at my foreign, bandaged self, but my stomach rolls at the memories of the girl's face and her fierce eyes. I haven't seen her since I fell into her. I hope she's gone forever.

My father runs through the voicemail messages. Dom's deep voice carries through the house, saying that he's calling to check on me. That he hopes I'm okay. He's miserable. He says he's sorry . . . so sorry . . . and that he tried to see me in the hospi —

My father jams his finger into the delete button and Dom's voice is gone. I think I'm supposed to feel something, but I'm strangely removed, numb. It's been this way since I woke up. I wonder if these are aftereffects of the LSD or if it's just . . . me now.

My father makes maybe three or four passes back and forth across the room without once looking at me, as if by not acknowledging me, he can make everything go back to normal. His withdrawal feels like punishment. And his agitation scares me. He's like a loaded gun. Looks like he could go off at any minute.

Finally he approaches me but doesn't sit. His stance is military. Feet spread. Hands on his hips. He gazes down at me with impassive gray eyes. "These antics of yours, they're going to stop."

I nod.

"You know what we're dealing with here. As a family, we're facing the very real possibility of losing everything. You copy? You have got to rein yourself in. You're our child, Ryan, but you're clearly old enough to fuck up your own life. If that's what you're determined to do, I have no doubt you will do it, but not under my roof. As long as we are responsible for you, you will submit to weekly drug testing. Stay away from Dominix for a while. He's been a bad influence on you. You will have a curfew of twenty-one hundred hours every night, and . . . no more senseless stunts."

"Understood."

This simple acquiescence from me seems to agitate him more, because he runs one hand over the top of his head and glares. "Don't play games with me, young lady. What you've done is serious. On top of endangering yourself with that jump, you've begun tampering with drugs. Your own actions landed you in the hospital and nearly killed you."

"I'm not playing games with you. I'm done with all of that."

He blows out an exasperated breath. I'm not sure why he

doesn't believe me. It's what he wants to hear, but it's also the truth. He turns and marches to the kitchen. Ice clinks into a glass, which he then fills with Maker's Mark.

Ayida watches him with her lips pursed together. "Nolan, do you really—" One look from him silences her before he disappears from the room. When she glances at me, her eyes seem to accuse—*look what you've made him do*—before she packs the expression away.

I push myself to standing. "I'm going to my room."

"Need anything?"

"No, thanks," I say, though that's not true. I need a lot of things that only time will bring.

The bedroom is dark. It takes a second for my eyes to adjust. I swipe the switch with an uninjured patch of my hand. The room comes to life with a galaxy of lights. Fatigue pulls hard at me, but restlessness thrums like a pulse and keeps me moving around. I open drawers, finger stiff jeans and soft cotton T-shirts, sniff various fragrances on the dresser. I'm so disconnected that everything seems foreign and new. Avoiding the mirror is easy: I'm still not ready to look at myself. I gingerly touch the gauze on my cheek and sigh. Whatever. I'm alive. That should be all that matters, right?

I want to sleep and see if I'll dream familiar dreams. The

bed is like open arms that I crawl blissfully into. Joe's hug comes to mind. I liked that hug.

It welcomed me back from the dead.

Because of the gash on my cheek, I can only lie on my right side. The numerous strings of mirrors and strands of lights above me sway in the slight breeze from the window. Their movement is reflected on the wall: planetary circles undulate on the white paint. My lids droop, but a whisper keeps me awake. When I force my eyes open, the many circles of yellow light on the wall are filled with the almond shapes of eyes.

I spring to my feet on the bed. My head plunges into the swirling vines of mirrors and lights. Each small cutout of glass holds a dark, fierce eye staring at me. I'm surrounded by the eyes of the ghost, boring deep into mine. Panic takes over. There's a scream like a shrill teakettle, and I know it's coming from my mouth.

Instinct moves my arms, swinging them through the fields of eyes, clawing to scratch them out. Lines of mirrors drop like spiders, covering my shoulders and body with eyes. Screaming, flailing, I'm attempting to fling them off me when strong arms grasp mine.

I swing again, catching something hard with my bandaged hand. "Ryan! What are you doing? What's wrong?" Nolan shakes me. "Calm down. Look at me."

"No," I moan, crying through lids that are squeezed shut. I can't open them, can't bear to see the haunting eyes that have fallen all around me. I collapse onto the bed and hug my knees to my face. There is tugging and pulling as my father tries to free me from the ropes of lights and strings of mirrors binding me to her.

"The eyes, the eyes. Make her stop watching me."

I hear Ayida's quaking voice from the foot of my bed. "What's happening?"

His voice doesn't shake like hers. It's a trained calm. The first sergeant is on duty, giving orders. "Call her doctor. I don't know what's wrong. I think she cut her eye. She's— she's crying *blood*. She was crazed, tearing everything off the ceiling. Could be a flashback from the LSD. Jesus, I don't know. Get them on the phone. Now!"

Quick footsteps retreat. He blows out one long exhale and whispers a whiskey-soaked statement from above me: "Goddamn. And I thought you scared me before."

TWELVE

"Do you think you can watch over your grandmother while I go to work for just a couple of hours?" Ayida asks a week later, during breakfast.

She looks haggard. None of us have slept too well recently. Me due to seeing those eyes every time I close my own. My mother because she wouldn't leave my side. My father because he hasn't had her by his. Gran . . . well, she hardly sleeps anyway. I think I have an inkling why: old people know their time is short and don't want to waste it sleeping. The best sleep I got was yesterday afternoon when Joe came over, sat silently next to me, and held my hand until I drifted off. When I woke, he was gone.

"I want to trust you," my mom ventures. Her eyes bear no trust. Especially since my newly appointed psychiatrist,

Dr. Collier, casually tossed around terms like *mental disorders, psychosis, phobias*. Now those words lie scattered on the floor around me like grenades, and we wait for Dr. Collier to pick one up and lob it at us.

Gingerly I take her warm hand. "I want to be trusted again. Go. It'll be all right." My stomach protests at the thought of being alone with my grandmother for a few hours. I have been tiptoeing around her ever since the incident. I want to be the strong version of me again, but I'm timid around her. She batters me with strange proclamations and opinions. It's like she hears every thought I don't voice.

There are so many thoughts I don't voice.

My mother clears the table and her throat. "We have another appointment with Dr. Collier this afternoon."

My teeth grind. I don't like his narrow pea eyes, which look like the wrong end of a telescope examining the deepest crevices of my brain. I'm playing nice, but I'll be damned if they're going to label me crazy. Dr. Collier has no idea what's in my head. Only Joe has any clue that I'm being stalked from a dark place in my reflections. Only I know that the more I see her, the more I'm sure she's trying to get inside me. Possess me.

As the thought of possession comes, I sense dark eyes on me. I'm being watched. Her angry presence swirls around the room as if my thoughts have summoned it. The hairs on my arms rise to points, and I shudder. It's terrifying to glance around the kitchen and know that our eyes will meet.

Not in the stainless-steel surface of the fridge, or the shiny teakettle on the stove, or the windows over the sink. My breaths come faster as I search. The eyes aren't in the glass surface of the table beneath my elbows, or the half-drunk bottle of water left on the counter. Anxiety fills me. I *know* the girl is with me. I feel her like shade over my life.

Mom comes over to kiss me goodbye, and I nearly recoil from her. The vengeful eyes reflect back at me through my mother's reading glasses. She removes them and sets them on her folded newspaper on the table next to me like a vial of poison. It's all I can do to not swipe them to the floor. I curl my hands into fists and smile.

She leaves, and the house suddenly feels both spacious and suffocating. I decide to seek out Gran, to see if I can cross our broken bridge and make things right. I find her sitting at the silent piano, staring straight ahead. Her head is bowed, gray hair pulled into a low, curly bun. She is so still, she looks as though she could be sleeping. Or . . . dead. My breath hitches. My steps are tentative as I approach with my hand outstretched to touch her shoulder. I want to be as far away as possible from the ice of death.

"Pancakes," she says, flinging her head up, which startles the ever-loving snot out of me. "I want pancakes."

"We just had breakfast, Gran." Every atom in my body vibrates faster.

"What difference does that make?"

Since I can't think of a difference, I don't answer. Sometimes you want what you want. I, of all people, should understand that. "Are you going to play something?" I ask.

Gran nods solemnly, places her fingers on the keys, and begins. A flash of memory pops in, that this is *her* song and that I was supposed to be listening for mine. My fingers twitch as I watch her play. I place my hands on the keys. There is a song in me, written on translucent vellum. It feels like it's been tied to a rock under a cold stream, but when my fingers touch the keys, it is freed, floating to the surface. I tap out the melody on the smooth keys. The song flows through me, stronger now; it moves my fingers without effort.

Gran snatches her hands back as if the piano has burned her. I keep playing, wishing she would watch my hands instead of staring at me with blind eyes. It's my hands and heart that are making music for her, not my bandaged face. But I'm glad that I've found a way to connect with her again.

"That's a hymn," she says when I finish. "'Just a Closer Walk with Thee.'"

There is no pleasure in her voice. It's something more like flabbergasted. This is not the reaction I expected. I thought she'd be delighted. "So?"

Papery hands caress both sides of my face. I cringe against the sting from her searching fingers over my wounded cheek, the bridge of my nose, my mouth. "So," she finally responds, "as far back as my feeble old mind can re-member, you've never played the piano." She scoots off the bench, the piano clanging loudly as she uses it for balance to stand upright.

I'm stunned. I can't explain what happened. "I know I seem different, Gran—"

"You *are* different, child. I don't need eyes to see that. I can feel it. You're wearing yourself like an ill-fitting coat."

Tears cloud my vision. Her wide back is still turned toward me, and it feels like a wall.

"It's true. Since the . . . *episode,* I've been struggling to feel normal. Do you know what it's like to play tug of war with yourself every day? I see things that I'll never be able to ex-plain. I've become afraid of everything. Afraid of life, even, because I know how easily it can be taken away. I don't want to live in fear. I hate it."

This burst of truth surprises me, and I wish I could reel the words back in before they're scrutinized.

The admission makes her turn to face me, and she sighs. "Everybody's got to clutch to their breast the things they're afraid to lose. You're smothering yourself. You used to be the wildfire—destructive, sure, sometimes, but *alive*. Now your fire has gone cold."

I hang my head. "That's sad."

"Certainly it is. Now, if you'll excuse me, I'm going to read on the toilet."

I stare after Gran's retreating form. She is both wise and wiseass. She's also right on the money. I want to carry my fire proudly, like the girl I was before, because right now I'm a tiny bulb plugged into a socket with too much voltage.

Per the note my mother left me, I go to the backyard to water the plants tucked into the bright orange ceramic containers that hang from the white stucco walls. Birds flit to the ground to splash in the puddles I've created. I like the peace back here, but I'm itching to hang out at the drop zone—to absorb the vibrant energy there. My dad probably isn't ready to be around me, though.

Dom has left two messages on our home machine, which I ignored like a well-trained soldier. I want to see Joe, but when I called, his mother said he wasn't home. She was very kind to me, though I'm sure she's wondering what kind of person I've become that I would take hallucinogenic drugs and end up in the hospital.

As I sit in a lounge chair, the quiet hum of insects, the birds, even the puddles' refracted surfaces—which make me uneasy, as all reflections now do—settle me into a zone where time becomes the coarse wind of the desert, eroding my hard edges.

I don't know how long I've sat out here. I might have dozed, though without fully sinking into sleep. Sleep has become a swamp I'm afraid to dive into. None of my dreams make sense. They are populated with strangers who want me dead, and the dream me is devastated.

I stretch and go into the house.

A black fly lands on the white marble of the kitchen counter where I'm writing in my journal. I've never kept a journal before, but everything is so jumbled, I need a place to smooth the gritty dunes of my thoughts. When another fly dive-bombs my ear, I swat at it and look up to see that the front door is wide open.

Gran has been very quiet since her . . . braille time. Too quiet. With a dry throat, I go to check on her.

First, her room. It must be said that no sane person would believe that anything but a voodoo priestess lives in this room. My grandmother follows the Obeah religion of the Caribbean. Knowing that doesn't prepare me for the broken glass and what looks like bird beaks in a bowl sitting on her bedside table. The smell is funky, like cigars and burning feathers. Gran looks like a big hat-wearin' Southern Baptist on the outside. But on the inside, she's . . . *witchy*. In a good way.

Fingering the charm bracelet she made for me this week to, as she put it, *ward against the loitering of foreign spirits,* I retreat backwards out of the room. *You and I were both born with the caul,* she said, referring to the rare veil of membrane over our faces when we were born. *For those of us with the veil, the spirit world is much easier to see. You're a strong young woman, but right now your strength is a sputtering candle, and I'm afraid for you.*

Eerie feelings quiver through me as I recall her words. I run out to search the rest of the house, with my chest constricting more by the minute. I call her name throughout the house and the backyard with no answer and no sign of her.

I'm running now, with no idea where she's gone except the wide-open front door. I fly through it and run smack into Dom. We collide like meteors, sparks and melting rock. His arms stay tight around me.

"Baby. Oh, girl. I've been out of my mind."

There are tears in his voice as my face presses against

his chest. I hear Dom's heartbeat. Do people know what a lullaby their heartbeats are? Life has many sounds and chords, but none are possible without the drumming of the heart. I lean into it like a baby in its warm, watery womb. It feels so good to be held.

He pulls my head from his chest, and for some reason all I can think of is us in the mirror. The vision of his hands on my lips and wandering over my body. It's surreal. I watch the trajectory of his eyes and notice them land on the large bandage on my left cheek. There is no narrowing of his eyes or fear that I'm forever changed. I'm grateful for that. But I've changed in ways he can't see.

"Nothing is more beautiful than you standing here. I thought you were dead," he barely chokes out. "I'm so sorry."

"I know," I say. Because what else is there to say? It isn't fair to blame him for my choices. I square my shoulders. "You know I can't see you anymore." I expected it to hurt the first time I saw him, I expected it to hurt to say those words, but I'm shocked that I don't hurt. I'm ice-cold. Numb.

Dom steps back like I've hit him.

"My father—"

He waves his hand. "It'll blow over with your father. I just came from speaking with him. He's still pissed as hell, but damn, he knows as well as anyone that you are your own woman. I've apologized for putting you in the situation in the first place. He knows you make your own choices, babe. Even when it comes to seeing me."

I pull away from his warm arms. "I can't deal with you — us — right now. I have an emergency. I can't find my grandmother. She's vanished. I have to go look for her."

"I'll help you."

I sigh. It's exactly the right answer but also the one that will get me into trouble. However, I'm more scared for her than I am for myself. "Okay. Thanks. Let's go find her."

We speed away on his motorcycle because that's all he's got and my car keys have been confiscated. The road leading to my house is paved, but that's being kind. I wonder if they just poured concrete over the jutted dirt and called it good. The desert stretches out around us for miles. If she wandered off into the waving heat . . . I swallow hard and push the thought away. My teeth rattle over the bumps, each one making me grip Dom's waist tighter. I want to close my eyes and lean into his back, but I've got to keep watch. "A bit more," I yell to him. "Then we should turn around and check the other way."

As I'm about to tell him to do that, I see the flash of police lights ahead. My stomach churns like I've swallowed squirming parasites that live off stress. Dom must notice too; the motorcycle speeds up. I breathe a little easier as we approach, because my grandmother is standing next to the patrol car, speaking animatedly with one of the officers. Thank God she's okay.

Dom holds out his hand to help me off the bike. "What's that on your grandma's chest?" he asks as I swing my legs over the seat.

It's not clearly visible from where we're standing, and the cop keeps blocking my view, but it looks like a large white paper hangs over her ample bosom. I run over to the other officer, whose face is pink with a sheen of sweat. "That's my grandmother. Is she okay?"

The cop nods and swipes his brow with his forearm. "Thankfully, yes. But she shouldn't be wandering around out here alone. This *is* the desert."

"I know." Oh God. I'm so busted. "I don't know what she was thinking."

"Oh, I do," the cop says in an amused voice. "We found her hitchhiking." He points to the sloppily written sign on Gran's chest, which I can now read: *IHOP or Bust.*

Gran's hands wave around as her prickly tone carries across the sand. "Unless you boys are going to take me out for pancakes with raspberry sauce, I'm not going any-where." You can tell this stalemate has been going on for some time, because the officer hangs his head in defeat. I'm guessing they don't make a habit out of forcing little old blind ladies jonesing for pancakes into the back of their patrol car.

I go in for the rescue. "Gran," I say soothingly with my arm around her shoulder, "let me get you home. We can make pancakes there." All eyes rove to Dom and his souped-up motorcycle.

"You don't have a car," Officer Obvious states.

"I'll take her on the bike." When multiple eyebrows rise, I realize how absurd it sounds. I put my hands on my hips. "What? I can ride it. I've done it before."

Dom laughs nervously. "What she means to say, *officers,* is that she's ridden with me lots of times. Since she doesn't actually possess a license for a bike" — he shoots me a look — "*clearly* she cannot drive her grandmother home. I think we should call your parents, Ry. Or maybe these fine officers won't mind giving you two ladies a lift?"

"I would like that young man to take me home on his motorbike!" Gran exclaims. When one of the officers starts to object, she holds up her hand. "Do not get on my nerves. I am a grown woman and I know my rights. I've been denied things because I am black. I've been denied things because I am a woman. And I've been denied things because I am blind. Damn it, I've been denied pancakes! By golly, you won't deny me this." She shoves past the officer toward the general location of Dom's voice. "I can sit on the back for one little mile, yes I can."

Both officers shrug their shoulders, probably glad for the oddball situation to be over. But one guy gives me a stern look as he flips his notepad closed. "Keep a better eye on her from now on. Would you like a ride back to the house?" he offers.

"No, thanks. I'll walk."

Dom looks at me helplessly as one of the policemen gives Gran a hand getting on the bike. "I see who Ryan takes after," Dom says to her. She wears a huge smile and claps like a little girl when he starts the bike up. Her plump cheek presses to his back, and she wraps her arms tightly around his middle. I watch the clouds of desert sand kick up as they putter slowly down the road, the wake of her laughter trailing behind. I walk through their cannon smoke of dust.

Something rustles behind me, and I spin around.

A tangle of sagebrush rolls past like it's running from something. Each tumbling scrape on the dusty road is a whisper.

How could you?

My legs twitch with the urge to run, but the brush and the phantom voice are rolling *toward* my house. So I stand stone still, barely breathing, and wonder if I'm imagining the things I've seen and heard.

How could you?

I remain motionless, frozen with fear as the desert breathes, unfazed, around me, until the sagebrush and the voice fade to nothing in the distance.

When I finally arrive at my driveway, lightheaded and jumpy, Dom is walking out the door with a miserable expression. His face is like a fierce angel from a painting—powerful, unyielding, but soft, too. He throws his leg over the bike seat. His tortured dark eyes smolder with cinders of a sad truth.

"Your grandmother told me that if I really loved you, I'd be gone before your parents show up."

Gran's right, of course. I'm already in enough trouble. It wouldn't help for them to find him here. He sits on his bike, waiting for me to say or do something. I'm not sure what he wants from me until he softly clasps my hand and pulls me to him, burying his face in my hair. He inhales, breathes me in. "Real love doesn't leave. It stays put."

My face stings where it's pressed against his T-shirt. I feel a fight in me: my promise to my father versus the familiarity between Dom and me. Passion is there, like a coal buried deep in my stomach that refuses to burn to ash. But

I don't feel the pull to him that I should. Every memory I see of us together taunts me like a book I wish I could live in but know I can't. There's that drumming heart again, but it's a melody I can't appreciate the way I'm supposed to. I'm not crazy. I'm not. But I don't understand why my emotions don't match my memories.

Why don't I feel anything?

Resigned not to hurt him any more, I decide I must tell him that we need a break. *I* need a break, until things are clear.

Still resting against his chest, I open my eyes and yelp. It's impossible that I will ever get used to her appearing. She shocks me, rippling mirage-like from the motorcycle's round handlebar mirror. Electric currents of fear rove over my skin. Her eyes, my eyes, are full of pain, watching our embrace. I stumble out of his grasp. "You — you can't love me anymore."

Dom holds up his arms in supplication. "What? You don't get to tell me I can't love you. I do. You know I do. More than anything, Ry. Besides my brother, you're all I've got. We screwed up, made a colossal mistake. Don't let it break us." He pierces me with his astute gaze, perhaps seeing for the first time how altered I am. "Don't let it break *you*."

THiRTEEN

Don't let it break me?

I'm already broken. Mashed up, like I've been pushed through a steel strainer. The cuts aren't just on the outside. I'm cut on the inside, too. I'm afraid of my own reflection. I'm afraid I don't know what's real. I'm afraid to touch the shiny brass knob on the front door for fear the surface will become a face. I close my eyes and turn the knob, envying Gran's blindness. I can't tiptoe through life wondering when my ghost will appear.

But you will.

The words ring out loud, spoken as a bitter promise, but I don't know if they've come from me or *her*. I will myself to stay calm. If I react, if I stumble every time I hear her voice or see her face, people will feel like they have to follow me around with their arms outstretched.

Gran is slumped in a large chair in the living room with the sun on her back. Tufts of hair escaped her loose bun during the motorcycle ride and hang like streamers around her face. I move behind her, gently pull the soft strands back and tuck them in, hoping she doesn't feel my hands shaking. I need to touch something real. It's a few moments before I trust my voice to speak. "You want me to make pancakes, Gran?"

"No need. We just ate breakfast," she says, as if I'm silly to offer. It's late afternoon, with the sun baking the desert into a hard crust outside, but I don't correct her. All the excitement has probably worn her out, created a swirling dust devil of thoughts in her head.

"Did he go?" she asks, and I think I'll never know how her brain slides so quickly from muddled to lucid, though more and more I know how she feels. Honestly, I was hoping she'd forget the whole episode so my parents would never have to know I lost her for a while. Wouldn't have to know they can't trust me.

"Yeah. He left."

"What's troubling you? Speak on it."

Besides almost losing her to the desert, hearing whispers on the road, and seeing the face of a ghost? I tell her the only thing I can. "I'm not sure about anything anymore. Even Dom. He's . . . intense." I haven't moved from behind Gran. Seems easier to talk freely from behind her.

"Mmm-hmm." She chuckles. "Like a certain girl we all know."

She pats my hand, which is now resting on her shoulder. "Only boy a girl like you is safe with is Joe." This makes her erupt into laughter, bobbing forward, slapping her knee. Laughter is pushy, tickling you from all sides, until you're infected with it. It feels good to laugh. Yet the thought that burrows in my brain, waiting for the laughter to subside is: *A girl like me?*

"That's a good sound." My mom's voice comes from behind. She plops her straw bag on a chair and kisses both Gran and me on the cheek, then gives me an appraising look. "Might want to throw a wrap over that hair," she says. "You haven't let it go so wild since you were a small thing."

I touch my hair self-consciously, unable to remember the last time I looked at it. Mirrors haven't exactly been my friend.

"We'd better head out soon for Dr. Collier's office. Besides, I don't think any of us want to be here when your father gets home. They raised prices again on aviation fuel. This world is conspiring to drive us out of business."

"What would we do then?"

"Oh, honey, I'm sure we'd figure something out, but I don't want to think about what that would do to your dad. That place saved him." Ayida grabs Gran's hands and helps her up. "C'mon, Mama. Let's get you ready to go." Her eyes narrow. "You look tired. What excitement have you two had today?"

My stomach clenches.

"Ryan played me a song on the piano."

My mother's eyes widen. "Did she, now? You finally wore her down, eh? Extraordinary."

"It was that, yes," Gran says with an ill-omened tone.

After a bit of fussing over what to bring to entertain Gran during my appointment, we head to one of the only psychiatrists in this small, impoverished desert town. Dr. Collier opens the door and asks my mother to speak privately.

"Are we here about me or you?" Gran asks the question so loud, it's like she thinks the answer is stowed in my ear.

"Me," I grumble while pretending to read a tabloid. I hope the specter doesn't make an appearance during my appointment.

My turn comes, and I perch myself on the edge of his couch. His eyes take in my body language. He must notice that I look like I'm ready to spring.

"Make yourself comfortable, Ryan."

I scoot my butt back, like, half an inch, unaware that I'm fiddling with one of the bandages on my arm until he looks down at it. He notices everything. "I know it's protocol to go through this, but we're all wasting our time. I'm not mentally ill. It was a stupid mistake. Stupidity isn't an illness." I clear my throat.

"I'd like to talk more about what happened the night you returned from the hospital. Your mother indicated that you had some kind of *episode*?"

Memory of my bedroom full of eyes bears down on me. My face flushes, making my cheek throb. This office is too hot. My mind squirms under his scrutiny. I feel like a bug that's been pinned to a board while it's still alive.

"I was tired."

"I'm sure you were. You'd been through quite a lot." He jots something down on a yellow legal pad. "You mentioned seeing eyes. Your parents said you wanted them to stop watching you?"

"I'd been sleeping. I had a bad dream, and I think I woke confused."

"You were dreaming that eyes were watching you?"

I swallow loudly. "Yes."

"You were standing and fighting with your eyes open," he says in that question-but-not-a-question way. I don't confirm or deny. He forges on. "And during your episode when you were on LSD, did you see eyes then, too?"

"Eyes . . ." I start to say yes, but that's not the whole of it. I saw a girl in the mirror. She saw me. We fell into each other.

I'd never been in a fight before that.

"You fought the eyes?" the doctor asks, scribbling.

I hadn't realized I'd spoken that out loud. "I was on drugs," I stammer. "Seeing things. Isn't that normal when you're on LSD?"

Dr. Collier scratches his head with the tip of his pen and smirks. "It's possible that what you experienced in your bedroom was what is known as a flashback. This can sometimes happen after taking psychedelic drugs. It's very important to let someone know if it continues, Ryan. You have nothing to be ashamed or afraid of."

You do. Yes, you do. Be afraid.

My head snaps up. Her threat echoes so loud, I wonder if he's heard it too. I glance at the window. His gaze follows mine. There is no face in the glass, just the frozen arms of a cactus outside. My heart thrums in my ears.

Be afraid, she says again.

He has no idea about my fear.

"And how are your emotions? Would you say you're feeling the normal range of emotions?"

"I'm not feeling much. My emotions are . . . deadened."

You should be dead.

Inside my sneakers, my toes are curled so hard they hurt. My hands are shaking bad enough that I stuff them under my legs. The voice has cast a spell on me. The rest of our session is like a bad date. There are too many questions on his end, too many one-word answers on mine. I figure the less I say, the better. Ayida bookends my appointment with another five minutes alone with the doctor, and then we're on our way home to make dinner. Gran has fallen asleep in the backseat. My mother is as rigid and silent as a tombstone.

Nolan is relaxing in front of the television, drink in hand, when my mom and I walk in, supporting Gran by her arms. She's a little wobbly from waking up, tipping like she's boozy. "Can we ride the motorbike again?" she asks through a yawn. I bite my lip, but my mom seems to take this as a dementia moment and answers, "Not just now, Mama. We need to make dinner."

We settle Gran in a chair by the kitchen table and get to prepping food. The doorbell rings, and I offer to get it so my mother won't have to.

Avery smiles and leaps on me for a tight hug. It's the first time I've seen her since the night of the LSD. "You're okay!" she squeals, then pulls back to look me over, taking in my bandages. "*Are* you okay? How bad is it?" she asks, pointing at my face.

"I don't know yet. It hasn't been *unveiled*."

"Well, what's a few scars as long as you're alive and well, right?" She bounds through the front door and hones in on the savory smell of caramelizing onions wafting from the kitchen. "I wanted to wait until things settled down before coming over," she says.

"Probably a good call," I say as my mom sets another place at the table.

My dad picks at slices of roast chicken faster than I can cut it. My mom shoos him away, but I can tell by her playful smile that she doesn't mind. There is warmth in gathering around the island, preparing dinner together. Family is the blanket that wraps us, even in dark times. I'm grateful for it. It's the first time I truly relax since I came home from the hospital.

Tension tiptoes into the room when my mom "accidentally" dumps my dad's drink in the sink, claiming she thought it was just melted ice. He pours another, a taller one this time. No ice.

"The date's been set for the mucky-mucks from the X Games," he announces. "We've got three weeks to get the place in shape." His drink sloshes as he motions toward me. "I'll need you to come in and shoot some promotional emails out to people. That's how you can help. We need a big push. If they do choose us, there's going to be some initial cost involved."

"Tomorrow, then?" I ask, excited to get out of the house. Excited that he needs my help in some way.

My mom's head snaps up from the peas she's shelling. "No skydiving."

"No question," my dad answers.

Now I feel two years old. "It didn't even need to be said," I say. "I'm not ready to go up yet anyway." As with my dad's "rules" speech, I'm being looked at like they don't recognize me, and I have to look away, continuing with my job of dicing the chicken.

My mom stops what she's doing and puts her arms around my shoulders. "Soon enough, baby. We know what jumping means to you." The blanket of love is once again around me. I tilt my head against her soothing arms. We could stay this way all night and I wouldn't mind. I've been starving for it.

A smoky shadow passes across the silver surface of the knife. I blink. I tell myself that it's our movements. I look again and see nothing but the glint of polished metal with bits of chicken clinging to the serrated edge. A sigh escapes me.

Softly, my mom kisses my cheek, and there's another

shadow in the shine, so fleeting, the quick flap of a bird's wing, the flutter of eyelashes, there and then gone.

Death . . .

The voice calls to me, as if that's my name. I shake my head. It's not my name. My name is Ryan. My name is Ryan Poitier Sharpe. My name is Ryan.

Death, she beckons again, and it occurs to me that perhaps she is telling me who *she* is.

I tilt the knife sideways to peer into it. My own eyes shine back at me, but then she rises out of them, glaring. I swing my hand upward, wanting to shake her loose. I want to make her disappear. I want her gone. I want her to know I'll fight her again. I'll win again. I wave the knife, slash at the air.

There's a yelp in my ear, and my father is on his feet, coming at me. I pull my hand back, away from him. My grandmother's head is tilted sideways, listening hard. Her fingers are over her mouth as she shoots to her feet, faster than I thought she could move. Avery's mouth is moving, but I can't hear her words through the ghost's murmurs. Pain sears through my shoulder as my father twists my arm painfully to the side.

Mine, Death whispers again, drawing my attention back to the knife that Nolan is trying to take from me. I'm scared for him, but I can't look at him. My eyes are focused on the blade, eyes locked with hers, which are crinkling with humor.

Death is smiling.

Mine.

"Do you hear her?" I scream. She's so loud. They must hear her.

From behind me, Ayida screams again. I crane my head to see her. Why are they looking at *me* like I'm the monster in this kitchen? Fingers pry mine open. The knife crashes onto the white floor—it's splattered like scarlet poppies in a field of snow.

A big, black boot smashes down on the knife. I wouldn't pick it up anyway. Nolan watches me, one arm stretched out to keep me back as he slowly bends down and slides it out from under his boot. He doesn't take his eyes from me as he asks Ayida, "Are you hurt bad?"

"N-n-no," she says through tears. "Small cut."

My head whips toward her at this. "You're cut? Oh God. No. She cut you?"

"She?" my father screams. His hands, still holding the knife, are on my upper arms. He shakes me so hard, my teeth rattle. I can smell the sharp tang of alcohol wafting from him. It takes me . . . somewhere else. "What the hell are you talking about? You cut your mother!"

My body goes limp in his grasp, gravity pulling me to

the floor so that my father is no longer shaking me; he's holding me up. "Are you telling me I have a crazy kid now?" His voice climbs, and his question suspends from the ledge of a mountain.

"Nolan, no!" Ayida pleads. She is upon us now; her hand, slippery with blood, grasps my arm, turning my bandages pale red. "She didn't mean to."

My mother and I are both crying. I'd cover my face, but my father hasn't let go of me. The pressure of his fingers feels like a pulsing vise around my arms. "I don't know what's happening to me," I cry. "Help me."

The voice is there again. I can't shut it out.

It screams. *Help me!*

FOURTEEN

"IT IS NOT UNCOMMON for a latent psychological illness to surface after the use of hallucinogenic drugs. More common, however, is drug-induced psychosis." Dr. Collier's deep voice resonates, bouncing off the shiny tiles in the house. My parents called him immediately after I wigged out in the kitchen, and he rushed over.

Nolan's voice eclipses Dr. Collier's. "Since she took it, she's been seeing things, hearing things. If it walks like schizophrenia and talks like schizophrenia—"

Dr. Collier interrupts him. "It hasn't been conclusively proven that taking LSD causes schizophrenia, and that's a diagnosis that takes some time. The same neural pathways—like roads in our brains, if you will—are stimulated, making the symptoms remarkably similar. Additionally, if a patient already has a marked lack of self-identity, they may, through use of hallucinogenic drugs, invite other *selves* in, so to speak. It's possible your daughter was already mentally unstable before taking the drug."

My mother speaks. "Ryan is the most self-identified person I know," she says through a wry laugh. "But this all started *after* she took the LSD."

That's not true.

"So," Dr. Collier says, "you saw no signs of instability, strange behavior, or mental distress in Ryan before the incident?"

I lie on my bed and listen to the painful beat of silence hanging after the doctor's question. Gran snores in a chair next to me, and Avery sits at my feet. She's reluctantly been assigned to watch over me while my parents talk to Dr. Collier.

"Is he suggesting that there was a mental illness lying in wait inside your brain?" Avery whispers, looking sideways at me like I suddenly make her nervous. "God. That's like having a bomb in your head and not knowing when it'll go off."

I shove Avery's thigh with my big toe. "I'm *not* mentally ill."

"Looks like I didn't wait long enough for things to settle down," she mumbles. "I know you do a lot of things for attention, but this is over-the-top."

I bury my face back in my arms. I *know* what I'm seeing and hearing is real. The face that follows me around may show up in flat reflections, but she's as three-dimensional as I am, as if I could reach in and touch her. I shudder. I *have* touched her. Every time she appears, she watches me with emotions pouring from her eyes like tears. Her eyes are angry, and I'm the nexus of her focus.

I cheated Death. Now she won't leave me alone.

Why is she so persistent, though? She'll have me eventually. She visits everyone at some point. Death always gets her way in the end.

"How do you know you don't have a mental illness? Do crazy people *know* they're crazy?" Avery asks. "And I don't mean to be rude, but you smell crazy. Like, when was the last time you showered?"

"Shhh," I hiss. "Don't upset the crazy person. I'm trying to listen."

Dr. Collier is speaking again. "Is there any history of mental illness, such as paranoid schizophrenia or bipolar disorder, in the family? Addictions?"

There is a heavy silence where I'm sure my mother's eyes flick to my dad. *Addictions.* But post-traumatic stress disorder is a response to something awful happening. Nolan has seen the ravages of war, has had his body permanently disfigured. I wouldn't call that a *latent* psychological illness.

I look over at Gran. Her mouth is slack, fingers twitching occasionally in her sleep. She's old, not mentally ill.

My disc is scratched, sure, but that's my fault. I didn't have to do what I did that night in the motor home. That was when things went very wrong.

The doctor continues. "We cannot overlook the seriousness of tonight's incident, for your safety and her own. A sedative can be administered for the night, but I'd advise an appointment with me first thing tomorrow. Ryan may require antipsychotic medication."

Tearful murmurs from my mother follow Dr. Collier's pronouncement. My father's voice is loud and clear. "I don't care if you have to medicate her. Hell, I'm medicated. Whatever's going on, fix it. This is the last goddamned thing we need right now. Control this shit, doc."

"Nolan!"

Dr. Collier clears his throat, which he does a lot. "I am committed to doing that, Mr. Sharpe."

The adults come to my bedroom door. The way everyone moves toward me, like they're trying to corner a stray cat, makes me want to scramble off the bed and curl into a ball or extend my claws. "The doctor's going to give you something to help you sleep," my mother says. My father hovers over me with a look of fierce determination.

"No! You don't understand. This isn't my fault. I didn't

mean for this to happen. She was talking to me. I was trying to get away from her, from the eyes — the eyes in the knife," I protest. The room goes silent. When I see the distrustful, wary look on their faces and my mother's bandaged hand, I'm forced to remember that I'm the one who hurt her. She doesn't deserve to be hurt. The spirit appeared, but I was the one holding the knife.

My mom wipes her eyes with fingers that are smeared with dried blood. I relent and let the doctor pour the pills onto my palm.

"I'll stay with her until she falls asleep, Uncle Nolan."

Gran is woken up and led to the door but stops and turns her head my way. "I dreamed you were waiting for me when I die," she says, her Caribbean accent even heavier with sleep. My mom bites her lip to keep from crying.

Yes, die, girl, the malicious voice whispers to me. *I'm waiting for you.*

I can't react. Must hold still, even though I want to cover my ears and scream. I lie down and pull up the quilt that Gran's mother made many years ago on the island. It wraps me in the blues and corals of the tropics. Palm trees, fish, and the cascarilla plants they farmed for shipment to Italy to flavor Campari all depict the life of the family. There's something comforting about enfolding myself in what came before.

Avery tries to make small talk as the sedative tugs at my grasp on consciousness. It pulls hard at me. Whether it's taking me deeper into myself or away from myself, I don't know. My hold is slipping, and that's what scares me the most. I feel like I could float away.

"Dom is one mopey, lovesick bastard," Avery says. Her voice sounds far away. "He walks around the DZ with his sketchpad, drawing and scribbling. It's sad. You'd better pull yourself together and get back. There's a line of girls circling like sharks, who'd be more than happy to comfort him."

"Hmm," I mumble. It takes effort to talk. "He's hurting. Someone should comfort him."

"That's crazy talk." Her hand swoops to cover her mouth. "Are you saying you don't care if someone moves in on him?"

I can't answer. I loved him more fiercely and openly than I've ever loved anyone besides JoeLo. I gave Dom all of me. He was my first. Why are all of our memories in my head but disconnected from my heart? Pictures scroll by, but I feel no attachment to them. Instead of heartache at being separated, I am emotionless.

It's like I've been born again, without a heart.

The next morning, we drive in stony silence into town. My body feels a hundred pounds heavier. "You could cut the tension in here with a knife," I say, and realize too late what a careless thing I've said.

Nobody responds, but I can see Nolan's jaw working like he's chewing on a gristly piece of reply. I probably should keep my mouth shut.

We continue our slow bounce down the road to see Dr. Collier for his assessment and also to see my regular doctor, who is going to remove the bandages today. Any sane person would be more worried about the permanent disfiguring scars on her face, but all I can think about is how I'm going to manage to seal the vault around my mind.

What's completely frightening about the questionnaire Dr. Collier hands me when I sit down in his office is that I could check off nearly everything on this list.

> Yes, I have hallucinations.
>
> Yes, I've been guilty of skipping showers or brushing my teeth, but not on purpose. I just . . . I forget, until someone remarks on my appearance or my teeth feel like wool.
>
> Yes, there are strange things going on that I can't explain.
>
> Yes, there is someone else inside my head who no one else seems to hear.

Yes, I often feel void of emotion.

Yes. Yes. Yes.

There's no way I'm agreeing to any of this.

I'm not crazy. I know I'm not, and there's no way I can let them medicate me. Just the thought of medication causes the most severe case of nausea to rise from my stomach. My aversion to it feels phobic in intensity. Desperate. They can't flatline me. They can't turn me into the walking dead. Whatever they gave me last night has made me feel so untethered from my body that I fear I'll plummet right out of it. It's like I'm the rider on a horse with a loose saddle that keeps slipping sideways. I'm afraid it will take all the fight out of me, and I need my fight to combat *her.*

In order to keep from being medicated anymore, I have to convince them that what my mom suggested was true. What I'm experiencing are flashbacks from the LSD, and I need time. I just need time.

After the physical examination, the written test, and the doctor trying very hard not to look frustrated as I give him as little information as possible, I am led out into the excessively beige waiting area. I wonder if they purposely leave it colorless so as to not provoke emotions in people. The receptionist glances furtively in my direction every few seconds while shuffling papers as Dr. Collier talks to my parents privately. She's acting like she's not watching over me, but I know she is. Everyone is watching me.

My parents come out of his office, ashen-faced and grim. My dad gives a tilt of his head that conveys his displeasure.

"Well?" I whisper to my mother as we head to the next appointment right across the street.

"Honestly, Ryan, I don't know what you told him—"

"Or didn't tell him," my father interjects. They flank me as we walk: wingmen to the cuckoo bird.

My mother roots around her purse for something, then answers while dabbing fuchsia lipstick on her generous lips without a mirror. "He says he can't conclusively diagnose you at this point."

"You sound disappointed."

Ayida stops walking and whirls toward me. "I am not disappointed he didn't diagnose you with bipolar disorder or paranoid schizophrenia or any other mental illness! I am disappointed you weren't honest with him! I have no agenda but to see you well, to see you get back to yourself."

"You want that, don't you?" Nolan asks me. His voice is uncharacteristically gentle as he opens the door to the medical facility.

I enter, and my footsteps stutter on the gray carpet. It's familiar. Too familiar, but I can't say why. "I don't want to go in here again. This place treats people like walking germs."

My mother scowls. "Baby, you've never been here before in your life."

My lips purse together. I could swear I've seen this place — though maybe it was in my bad dreams. The memory is dreamlike, hazy. Haven't I previously shuffled down these long halls lined with enlarged glossy photographs of the desert? "You sure?" I ask. Walking the corridor is like being dipped in a vat of desolation. Every cell in my body rejects the idea of being here. I want to run.

"I'm certain." She points to the photographs. "You'd think they'd put up pictures of the beach or forests," my mom comments with fake cheeriness. "We see enough of the desert as it is."

"Pictures of the beach would just be a tease," I answer shakily, glancing at a black-and-white of a Joshua tree posing haughtily for the sun. I suck in my breath, seeing the spirit's face flash at me from the thick, gnarled branches in the photograph.

In the next picture — the sun setting behind the Sierra Nevada — her eyes pierce mine, her face as stony as the granite mountaintops. I force myself to keep walking.

A still photograph of a menacing, coiled, tawny rattlesnake makes every hair on my body rise. I will myself to stare at it. How can she possibly harm me? But it looks as though venom drips from her open mouth. The sound of the fast quiver of a rattler morphs into her scream. My skin rolls with fear, with the sensation of shedding, like that snake.

Do snakes feel fresh and vulnerable after they've discarded their old skin for new? How long does it take for the new skin to thicken so that sensations don't feel like an assault? My spit tastes like sour, acidic venom.

Photo after photo scrolls by, and there she is, in every frame. My heart pounds as if I've been running an endless hallway. The girl is determined, though. She tells me in a voice like the snarl of a leopard, *I will haunt you forever.*

I keep my head down until I'm sitting in the waiting area. My mother asks if I'm okay. Words will betray me. They already have. I nod and sit on my bandaged hands to conceal their violent trembling. We're ushered into the exam room. There are no mirrors, thank God.

First the doctor removes the bandages from my arms and upper thighs. I crinkle my nose at the yeasty smell of the gauze. Is it supposed to smell like illness? My stomach rolls. Something about being in this room makes me feel like my blood is pulsing thick with a spreading disease.

Then, slowly, she peels away the wide swath of cotton

gauze on my cheek. The air hits it with cool breath. I feel exposed. My mother's hand flings upward to her mouth, but Nolan seizes it and pulls it calmly to his side. She turns away from me and pretends to search for something in her purse.

"Bad, huh?" I ask my father as the doctor prods my cheek. He'll steel himself and tell me the truth.

"You're beautiful," he answers without averting his eyes from the lie. That small, unexpected kindness from him is enough to choke me up.

The doctor turns toward the cabinets and opens a drawer, telling me how to care for my wounds until they're fully healed. She turns back toward me and holds up a hand mirror directly in front of my face.

It's me and it's not me staring back. It's never *just* me. I thrust the mirror away, but the doctor wasn't expecting my reaction, and it clatters to the floor, fracturing into angular pieces. Dozens of different-size eyes stare up at me.

"Ryan, please stay calm." My mother wraps her arms around me. "It will heal. You're going to be okay."

The doctor tries to reassure me, telling me that it's always hard for people to adjust to facial scars but that it will heal and be much less noticeable over time. I hear only half her words before running out of the room, crushing eyes under my heels as I go.

FIFTEEN

THERE'S NO WAY they can catch me. It's painful for my
dad to run due to his war injuries, and my mother has
nothing on my long-legged speed. I had to get out of there,
out of the confining antiseptic of the medical building and
into the open air. It's exhilarating to run full-out like this,
the exquisite tension and release of every muscle doing its
job. Every breath is life itself inflating my lungs, coursing
oxygen through my blood. No matter my confusion, uncer-
tainty, and fears, I'm lucky to feel all of it. I'm lucky to feel
at all.

My heart pounds a cadence: *I'm alive. I'm alive.* Even *she* is
quiet right now beneath the thrum of it.

I zigzag through side streets and alleyways until my
body is running on fumes, the cut on my cheek throbs with
my pulse, and I come to a gasping halt on a street corner. I

need to call Joe. He'll come for me, sit with me, let me cry without explanation. He will look at me tenderly. He's the only person in this world who doesn't want anything from me right now that I can't give.

There are already three messages on my cell from my parents asking where I am, begging me to stay calm and let them come get me. Thankfully, Joe answers my call right away. I try to direct him to wherever I am. "I wasn't exactly looking where I was going," I say, giving him the street names of the intersection in the quiet neighborhood where I finally stopped.

There's something about the names that runs tickling fingers up my back. This neighborhood conjures an intense feeling of déjà vu. A knowing without knowing why. I venture a few feet down one beckoning street in particular, thinking I shouldn't go anywhere, but I can't seem to stop. The gentle dips and sways of the aging picket fences pull me along like the handrail of a bridge toward a mysterious destination. I glance back, looking for Joe, but I have to keep going; I have to know where the feeling leads.

Death is still quiet in my head, as if she's as curious as I.

All I can do is follow my feet, which plod a deliberate path to a vague end. With each step, my agitation builds. I'm simultaneously compelled to search and yet terrified of what I'll find. I don't understand this. As if I've reached a cliff, my feet scuffle to a halt. Rocks tumble over the edge of my mind as I stop and stare.

In front of me is a house. A modest, blah house on a modest, blah street. It's dilapidated and looks abandoned. But I can tell it was beautiful once. The grass is dead and sparse like residual hairs on a skeleton. Stapled to the door, the corner flap of an aged notice rustles in the hot afternoon air.

There is no life in this house. It's a shell of what it once was.

The memory of a death rises up. I recall thinking how a body looks so much smaller when there is no soul to fill the spaces: like a balloon, wrinkled, puckered, half-deflated on the hard, cracked ground. I find it alarming that I can't recall right now whose dead body I viewed. Do I know anyone who has died? My father has never let me see the bodies of the skydivers who bounced. Have I ever attended a funeral?

Tears drop onto my neck, surprising me, like a chaste peck of rain on the forehead. This house makes me inexplicably sad. I can't make sense of it.

A blaring honk startles me. I swing around. Joe leaves the car running as he steps out. His face shines with sweat and a frantic expression. "What are you doing over here? Why didn't you stay on the corner where you told me to go?

I've been looking all over for you." He clutches my upper arms, leans forward to kiss my cheek, pauses, and switches to the uninjured cheek. I'm directed to the passenger side of the car, where he opens the door, sits me down, and buckles me in like I'm two years old.

"I'm sorry." I don't know what else to say. I wasn't thinking, just following an indistinct trail, mindless, like a hound with the barest whiff of something it wants. A terrified thought rushes in: maybe *she* led me there, somewhere random and empty where people wouldn't be able to get to me until it was too late. Fear wraps its fingers around my heart and squeezes. That's why she was so quiet.

It's not a good sign when Death holds her breath.

"I'm glad you found me. Can we go now?" I say with a quaking voice. I want to be very far from this house, but Joe hasn't moved the car. He's busy punching a text into his phone. "What are you doing?"

"Letting your parents know I've got you."

I shake my head. "You're not going to hand me over. I need a break from them right now, Joe. That's why I called you." I curl my fingers over his hand on the gear. "I need you to distract me, take me somewhere where I won't think so much."

"I'm letting them know you're okay, which is what you should have done if you were thinking straight." He sighs, regret on his face. "Sorry. But everyone is worried about you, sister love."

"Don't take me back yet." I fix him with a hard stare. "I'm not asking."

He blinks his agreement, and we drive aimlessly for a while with the radio blasting, top down, and warm air filling the space around us. The desert smells like sage leaves brushed with rain, then baked. I've held my eyes closed since we left the abandoned house. My fingers catch the wind outside, first cupping and holding it, then flexing against it. The resistance hits my flat palms and I smile — muscle memory of dancing in air.

"Been to the drop zone much?" Joe asks, as if he can read my mind.

"Not at all, actually."

"Might be good for you." The car comes to a slow stop, and I open my eyes to see he's pulled up at the airport. We bump down the dirt road adjacent to the landing circle. Out of habit I gauge the windsock, and a memory blows by. "Dom and I wanted to make a skydiving calendar of jumpers wearing only the windsock and maybe some jump gear."

"I know," Joe says. "You let him take sexpot pictures of you as a test run."

"Oh . . . that's right." He hands over a bag of pistachios,

and we recline our seats to watch for the jumpers. "Why don't you like him?"

"Why haven't you asked before? I've been wondering why my opinion didn't matter to you."

"My opinion mattered more, I guess."

Joe fights with a pistachio shell that doesn't want to open, gives up, and tosses it in the dirt. We both squint at the jump plane roaring past us down the runway before it leaps into the air. He is thoughtful but finally answers my question.

"A couple of years ago, my dad showed me how to use jumper cables on the car battery. He was adamant that I follow his instructions to the letter so I wouldn't blow up the car or myself or be burned by acid or something. I was freaking nervous. I'd be heading toward the battery with these cables and clamps like I was walking to the electric chair, imagining it zapping me and frying me crispy." He tosses more pistachio shells onto the ground. "You know the feeling when you're playing that game Operation?"

"I love that feeling," I answer, remembering the exact sensation of combined fear and excitement.

"Right. Well, the thing about you and Dom is, you both like that feeling a little too much. Though"—Joe chuckles— "you might be even higher on the need-for-adrenaline scale than him. Anyway, your love is a white-hot electric arc. I'm afraid you'll get burned by it."

Just as he says this, I see Dom walk out of the hangar. I know what it feels like to walk shoulder to shoulder with him. I remember the taste of his mouth after a long day of jumping, a mixture of sweat and excitement and his spearmint gum. I recall every word he's ever uttered to me about how remarkable and beautiful he thinks I am. I remember my own words of love and admiration back to him. I remember one night, lying on the grass behind the hangar and staring up into the sea of stars, I told him that I thought we were two halves of the same star. He called me his Lady of Light. Our fire burned the same. Later, he gave me a painting he'd done of a split star, with tendrils of light from the two halves still connected like they were reaching for each other. All of these are beautiful memories but not sensations. I should *feel*, but I don't.

I feel dead.

What the hell is wrong with me?

Avery jogs after Dom and follows, puppylike, at his heel. Her hands move excitedly as she talks. While his head is craned toward the sky and the airplane, hers is craned toward him.

"I think I have to let him go," I say, watching Joe's face for a reaction. I can't tell if this pleases him or not. For the first time in hours, though, the *spirit* reacts. I quaver like someone is grabbing the cage of my ribs and shaking them. My hands dig into the leather seat.

Joe suddenly points skyward. "There they go!"

The plane slows over the drop zone. Little by little, I'm able to make out the forms of bodies dropping. They're specks, dust motes in the shafts of light between clouds. One by one, parachutes open like falling blossoms against the blue sky. It's unbearably beautiful.

Joe pulls me in to his side and wipes my cheek. "Don't worry. You'll be up there again soon."

"I don't know—"

"Not hearing it. This watered-down Ryan can stay for a while, but sooner or later the real Ryan is going to come back to us, stronger than ever."

"She might be gone forever." I sniff, curling closer to his warmth.

"Only if you want her to be." We sit in silence like that, watching the skydivers float down to earth. Joe shoos me back to my side and starts the car. "I know what you need: some good old-fashioned fun. I need it too. I've missed you. You game?" When I stare at him blankly, he whispers, "The right answer is . . ."

I blink the tears away. "Always."

"That's my girl. Let's go."

SIXTEEN

WE PULL UP at Joe's house. The patch of lush green grass in front curls my toes with want. My mother says it's the Caribbean in us that makes our skin forever thirsty for green.

"Hello, Mrs. Lawrence," I greet the petite woman who's bent over a table, gluing colored shards of glass into a bright mosaic. She wipes her hands on her apron and hugs me tightly.

"What's this *Mrs. Lawrence* business, honey? Now, you come right in and sit down. Tell me how you're doing."

"I'm okay, I guess." Her shrewd brown eyes scan my face, my hands. She's watched me grow up, and I can see in her eyes that she knows how I'm doing just by looking at me. I'm getting used to that disenchanted downward flick of the eyes that says I'm less now. "I'm a mess, right?"

A weak smile. She's good enough not to deny the truth.

Joe grabs my hand and pulls me. "That's why we're here. Ma, do you have a robe we can borrow?"

"A robe? I need a robe for good old-fashioned fun?" I ask into his shoulder.

"Honey, no fun is gonna start with you — and I say this with complete and utter love — looking like you've been sleeping with bears on the Pacific Crest Trail for a month."

Joe scurries around, making lemon water, bringing me a plate of fruit and cheese, and running a bath overflowing with frothy bubbles. He unwraps a travel toothbrush and tosses it on the bed next to me with a look that says, *Scrub the ass out of your mouth this instant.*

I change into the robe and sit in stupefied silence at how he cares for me, and for the first time in a while I'm embarrassed by how I look, especially as Joe stands in front of me and assesses my hair. "I don't know what we're going to do with that gnarly 'fro of yours," he says, with his hands on his hips. "The fact that you've let it go like this worries me more than anything else. Let's start with the basics like water and shampoo and go from there."

"Can we cut it?" I ask, surprising myself.

His eyes widen. "You want to hack at that glorious mane of curls you're so vain about? That doesn't make me question your sanity *at all.*"

He takes me by the shoulders and walks me to the bath, slipping the robe off as we go. I smell how rank I am. I clutch the robe to me, and he laughs. "Modesty? You?" I bite my lip and step toward the tub. The scent of ginger wafts around me as I sink into the white blanket of bubbles. "Lean your head back." He pours a pitcher of water over my head. Having fingers massage soap into my hair feels luxurious and decadent. There is a cat deep inside me, purring with delight.

Joe leaves for a bit to assemble some kind of "suitable" outfit for me to wear. My scalp tingles. I wash the rest of me, thinking of the vulnerability Gran must feel every time I've had to bathe her. I haven't given myself much consideration lately. My body is foreign to me. Sticking my legs out of the bubbles, I admire the elongated power of my thigh muscles, the length of my legs, which stretch out beyond the end of the tub onto the white wall of the shower. I run my hand over my sinuous arms, even my long toes. Everything about me is stretched and strong.

The inside used to match the outside. Even Joe misses the old Ryan. He said so at the airport. It's the first time I can remember him wanting something I couldn't give. I'm so lost. Makes me want to snap my fingers and be that Ryan again, but I don't know how to begin. Perhaps it *is* time to skydive again. Something to jump-start myself.

My skin is tender around the healing cuts, so I gently pat myself dry and try to pull my fingers through my tangled hair. It's hopeless. "Joe?"

"Yeah?"

"Get the scissors."

His brows crinkle. "I'm not so sure—"

"You do it, or I will."

Snap.

He holds up his hands in surrender, but his pleased smile tells me he likes seeing a spark of my previous fire. "Fine, fine. It's only hair. I'll be right back." He returns moments later with a chair and scissors, and positions me in front of the mirror. I fist a hunk of my ringlets and clip them off, all the way to the scalp, in one snip. Cold air swirls around me. We are not alone in this tiny bathroom.

I hand Joe the scissors, flip the chair around, and sit. "Finish."

"Well, after that cut, I have to, just to make you look okay. Either that or you'll be wearing hats for a year. You don't want to watch?" he asks.

"No."

I don't want her watching me.

"I trust you," I tell him with a squeeze to his hand. "Make it really short." Nerves fire off in my belly as the metal blades slice together. A snarled ringlet coils on the floor. I close my eyes.

"I gotta say," Joe says, standing back and admiring his work. "It shows off your face. It's weird, though. You look three inches shorter without all the fluff on top." Skull and soft fuzz are all I feel when I rub my hands over my head. But when I turn around, I don't like what I see. "I look like a cancer patient," I say, swallowing inexplicable tears that rise up with those words.

Joe hugs me from behind. "You look like the rebel you are." Then his voice softens. "You look like a fresh start."

We hang for a couple of hours, watching a movie and talking until the sun dips below the mountains. He's pulled together a pretty cute outfit, though I still don't know where we're going. Jeans roll up my calves, a couple of tank tops are layered, and he wraps one of his mother's scarves over my newly shorn head.

"Where we're going, no one will care how you look." With that he hands me a cargo jacket and we wave his mom goodbye. This feels good. Some kind of normal. I was right to go with Joe; I needed to get out of my own head for a while.

Getting to the larger city of Palmdale is a bit of a drive. We pull into In-N-Out Burger, order Animal Style cheeseburgers and fries, then head to Joe's super-secret fun place, which is apparently located in a strip mall with a doughnut shop, laundromat, and nail salon. Small groups of guys and a few girls cluster around the front door. Intermittent flashes of light slide by as the door opens and closes. Music thumps from inside.

I clap my hands. "A dance club!" The excitement I feel is a welcome change. Misery begets misery as ... someone used to say. Who used to say that? It's another of those moments when memories feel as intangible as fog. Through the fog a man's voice spits lofty phrases and Bible quotes at me: *For I consider that the sufferings of this present time are not worth comparing with the glory that is to be revealed to us!*

"Easy for him to say. He wasn't the one suffering."

"What did you say?" Joe asks over the noise.

Rattled, I shake the thoughts from my head. "Nothing."

"This isn't just any club, sister. This place is my new discovery. You'll love it."

Our hands are stamped, even though we must look underage. No one seems to care, and when we enter, I see that we're not the only kids here. Forget talking. The music is loud. It thumps in my bones, reverberates deep in my chest, competing with my heartbeat. It drowns out every other sensation. I love the all-encompassing soak of sound and vibration.

Joe yells something into the din. "What?" I yell back.

Then he makes this exaggerated funky-dance face and swooshes his body around. He steers me up a small flight of stairs to an upper-level dance floor and grabs my hips from behind. Can I do this? I feel weedy, and the music is so powerful, it lashes against my tender skin. People's hands wave in the air, but no one else looks as I must look, as if the music is a snake charmer that's coaxing my skin over my head like a worn shirt.

After a few hesitant moments, I close my eyes, lean back against Joe, and let myself go. Just ride the music, forget everything in the past, and stop worrying about the future. I'm here now, wrapped in music and dancing with the best friend I've ever known.

I swing around to face him, resting my arms on his shoulders. He glances into my eyes briefly, but his eyes are too busy scanning the crowd to linger there. Familiar, this invisible feeling: it stabs me with antagonism. I place my palms on his face. He zeroes back in on me with a laugh. "Oh no," he hollers into my ear over the music. "I'm not falling for that one again."

I have the strongest urge to pull his face closer. Even as I'm wondering why, I'm tilting my head and brazenly grazing his lips with mine. When I open my eyes, his are narrowed, perplexed. His dancing has slowed to a sway. I press against him and kiss him again. His mouth is stiff, unresponsive to my lips. The walls of our teeth clank to-gether awkwardly.

Joe recoils, stunned. "You *meant* that!" he yells over the music. "Why would you do that?" There is accusation in his voice, in his eyes, which flash with anger and confusion.

"I don't know." I shrug. I really don't. But the feeling was so strong, I *had* to obey it. "Because . . . because I love you!" I yell over the music.

His head cocks to the side. "I love you, too, but it doesn't mean I want your tongue in my mouth. Jesus, Ryan!" Joe takes a couple of steps away but stops when he realizes I'm following him. He holds up his hand. "You're going to mess with my man magnetism." He shimmies a couple of feet away and melts into the mob of bodies glowing neon from the swirling lights.

Keep moving. By myself. Like an idiot. Dancing will keep me from feeling stupid and rejected. What I did was impulsive, but I followed an uncontrolled inner drive. I try to make sense of it. From the moment I woke up in the hospital, Joe was the one who made me feel some peace, belonging. He loves me. I love him. It seemed natural to show it, I tell myself. But the urge was beyond my consciousness. I keep dancing to forget the look on his face when I kissed him. I'm sticky with sweat and embarrassment.

The music thumps in my head, but I can still hear her voice as if we're alone in a dark cave. *Stupid bitch.*

An enormous disco ball rotates above the dancers. Blackness curls its fingers around my vision for a moment before letting go. Leaning forward, hands on my knees, I wait for it to pass. When I can focus, eyes are everywhere I look, swirling on the floor, ceiling, walls, spinning on the sweaty skin of other people. Everyone is tattooed with the eyes of Death.

"Hey!" snaps a girl when I grab her shoulder to steady my wobbly legs. The face is even behind my eyelids. I can't shut it out by closing my eyes like before. This, whatever this is, is getting worse. My body rebels, shakes violently; the saddle slips sideways even without medication. I don't have a hold on myself; I could fly out of this body into the darkness right here in the middle of this pulsing nightclub.

Louder than the music, I hear her laughing.

SEVENTEEN

MY KNEES AND HANDS slam into the gritty dance floor. It's an enormous effort to keep from passing out. Someone steps on my fingers. I force my eyes open. Her reflection, *my* reflection, sweeps over the floor in circles, over the shoes around me, over my hands as I try to push myself to standing.

This kind of thing can't happen, especially not in public. They'll size me for a crazy suit for sure. I crouch self-protectively with cold hands around my knees.

Swimming out of quicksand would be easier, but I finally manage to make it to my feet. I've done it. I'm stronger than she is. But my victory is short-lived. Joe sees me and begins his own swim against the crowd to reach me. He slides my arm over his shoulder and half drags me out into the tepid air of the night.

"This is all my fault," he says, putting me into the car. "You weren't ready."

I slump in my seat. "Am I ever going to feel normal?"

He squeezes my thigh. "It's okay. It was my grand dumbassery to push you. You'll come around."

Maybe this is what they mean by the phrase *bleeding heart*. My heart bleeds to hear Joe's longing. He shouldn't blame himself. He just wants his best friend back.

"What happened in there anyway?" he asks. "You looked like you were going to faint. Were you seeing things again?"

I rub my hands over my nearly bare scalp and hide my lie with a smile. "No. A little dizziness. It's been a big day." We're silent during the drive home. What is there to say, anyway? How I don't know who I am, and how no one else does either?

Joe motions toward my house when we pull in the drive. "Whoa. What's going on here?" The headlights illuminate my grandmother stooped over in front of the house. With one hand she is using the wall of the house to guide her as she walks the perimeter. Her other arm is swaying back and forth rhythmically, as if she's sprinkling seeds on the ground. Her dress snags on a cactus, and she impatiently tugs it away, ripping the hem.

"Does she normally garden at night?" Joe asks.

"Gran does a lot of weird things, but from the looks of it, I don't think she's gardening."

My mother is clearly trying to coax her inside. She motions for help when she sees us running over, but soon her face morphs into baffled shock. "What in God's name have you done to your hair?"

Realizing Joe's mother's scarf is gone, I open my mouth to answer.

"Never mind. Help me get your grandmother in the house," she says, as if we have superpowers or are supposed to jump Gran and manhandle her inside. I see now that it's not seeds Gran is sprinkling along the edges of the stucco walls but grains of white rice.

"Why are you throwing rice on the house, Gran?"

"Is there even an answer that will make sense?" Joe whispers. "I think it's a little late in the season for rice planting."

Gran's head snaps up at this. "Don't talk like I'm soggy in the brain. I'm not planting rice, fool. I'm protecting all of us!"

"From?" I barely utter. My heart contracts like it's hiding.

"The *duppies,*" she answers with a dramatic urgency that makes my hairs stand on end. Summer wind whips her nightdress, wraithlike, around her calves. "The spirits who roam at night. They have to count all the grains before they can enter the house. I'll put down so many they can't finish counting before sunrise." The lines in her face are etched into a map of determination as she flings my mother's restraining hand off her arm.

Joe throws up his hands. "I was totally wrong. That makes perfect sense."

I stomp on his foot. "Is there a dimmer switch on your blurting button?" I whisper back to him. "Gran, are you afraid there are bad spirits trying to get into our house?" I attempt to keep my voice as steady as possible.

At my question, she stops sprinkling rice against the base of the house and shuffles toward me. Her hand arcs in a half circle around each side of me. Rice pellets my sneakers. She answers with her dead eyes fixed on me. "Child, I'm afraid they already have."

Shivers roll down my arms. An exasperated sigh escapes my mother. "Go on in," she tells Joe and me. "It's no use. I'll stay with her until she's finished."

Joe grabs my hand and we jog to the front door. Gran's absolutely right: spirits have already penetrated these walls. The first thing I see upon entering the hall is a mirror. Shining back at me is the tortured spirit who haunts my reflection. Her face undulates in the glass, rippling against an unseen wind. Her eyes bore into mine with ferocious determination.

I've had enough. Joe calls after me as I run down the hall to the linen closet. I heap sheets and towels into my arms, run back to the entryway, and fling them onto the floor. I take one white towel and drape it over the mirror, covering her malicious face.

How will you stare at me now? I ask her in my mind. She's clever, though. Mirrors are just one way she imposes on me. It's like she's tethered to my body by an invisible cord, following me, part of me, always. I want to cut her out, excise her forever.

"Ryan?"

Joe's voice sounds far away. I run to the couch and stand on it to reach the upper corners of the mirror above it, carefully covering it with a large sheet. The world is a maze of carnival mirrors with her face always watching. I'm sick of it. Now my father's voice funnels in from behind me. He's asking in the same panicked tone as my mother about my shorn hair. I ignore both of them, because I'm sure if I don't find a way to stop her from stalking me, I really *will* go crazy.

"Did something else happen?" I hear my father ask Joe.

"No. I mean, she got dizzy when we were out, but . . ."

I run to the piano and throw a blanket over the varnished, black surface.

"Why is she covering the mirrors? Is she seeing things again?" my dad asks.

"I — I didn't know you knew about that," Joe stammers.

"Of course. She's been seeing things ever since she over-dosed. That's when this all started."

There is a pause, substantial enough to stop me. I remember telling Joe about seeing the faces before the LSD. He *can't* tell my father that. It's the only thing keeping them from medicating me: the idea that, with time, the effects of the drug will fade away and I'll be normal again. I give Joe a warning look and toss a tablecloth over the glass dining table. Joe will keep my secret.

"No, sir. No, that's not right."

I swing around. "Joe!" When he looks at me, I know I can't stop him from saying what he's about to say. "Please."

"She was hallucinating before the LSD." He's speaking to my father, but his eyes never leave mine. "She told me about it before she ever did the drugs."

I mouth the word *Why?*

"Because I love you. And because you taught me how to be brave, and sometimes that means that I'll have to piss you off. It doesn't help you for me to lie. Your parents should know the truth."

"I'm not crazy! A ghost is stalking me, trying to possess me!"

"Oh, 'cause that's sane!" Joe yells.

"You're only doing this because I tried to kiss you!"

My father rubs his face with both hands. "*Why* would you try to kiss Joe?" he asks as if this is the craziest thing he's heard all night.

I'm whirling with thoughts, some mine, some from an unseen place I can only assume she inhabits. "I don't know!" I scream. "I thought, I mean, love . . . I've been numb to every good feeling, but I feel love with him."

Nolan takes a big swig of his drink. "You want to love a guy romantically who loves guys, Ryan? That doesn't make sense. He's gay."

Joe steps toward me, his hands curled into hard balls. I have no memory of him ever looking so livid. "You think your feelings override who I am? Override *gay*?"

"But gay is an abomination!" As soon as I've said it, I feel inside like Joe looks on the outside, as if we've both been punched in the gut. I cover my mouth. Somewhere within me, I knew. But it's like I forgot the truth about Joe in the midst of my confusion.

I don't believe what I just said.

Joe's jaw is clenched tight as he responds. "You expect parents to be ignorant asses, their visions of the perfect child dashed by our annoying tendency to be different from them. But you . . . you turning on me now hurts worse."

My father is background scenery as Joe and I stare at each other. I feel as though I should avert my eyes, but he's the only person I've felt any real emotion for since I reentered this world. I don't know how I got it so wrong. I feel like I've spoken someone else's words.

Finally Joe says, "This you . . . and me . . . we'd have never been friends."

His words slice right through me. He's out the front door and gone. Like that, my best friend is gone.

A hurricane of fury blows through me. Beneath my hands, under the white cloth, the table fractures like a gigantic slab of ice. Glass and my heart shatter to the floor. I stagger back. "I didn't do that," I say to my father, who's rushed over. "I swear I didn't break it. How could I? It had to be *her*. You have to believe me!"

"I believe you need serious help, and—like I was—you are too damn sick to know how badly you need it."

"If you've decided I'm sick, then nothing I say has any credibility. Nothing I tell you matters."

I take a step toward him, but glass crunches under my shoes and I halt. His eyes snap down to the fractured table, then back up to my face.

"Nothing you tell me will matter more than what I can see with my own eyes."

"What about what I see with mine?"

Nolan doesn't answer me. My question hangs in the air before dropping to the floor with the other broken pieces.

EiGHTEEN

"A fear of reflections often reveals that there are things you don't want to see about yourself, hence the covering up of all the mirrors in your house. Spectrophobia is the fear of mirrors. It's possible that you may be suffering from this phobia, Ryan. Therapy and medication have proven useful to overcoming it."

I don't respond, just openly scribble in my journal, which I've begun to carry everywhere because I'm assaulted by random images and daydreams that feel more like memories. The night dreams are worse. Five nights of hell since the fight with Joe. Days and days battling a ghost only I can see. Gran's rice didn't manage to stop that.

Writing in front of Dr. Collier without showing it to him is a statement. My thoughts are my own. Besides, I have to capture the dreams I had last night before I forget them.

It's always the same. People want me dead. People I love but do not recognize. In the dream I always feel utterly abandoned.

Except for my pen moving across paper, the room is so quiet the carpet makes sounds, rustling like dry wheat.

"Is there anything that you feel ashamed of? Anything about yourself that you'd rather not look at?"

I glance up from my journal. "In your opinion, is everyone crazy who believes in ghosts?"

"Does your scar trouble you?" Dr. Collier asks, pointing toward his own cheek with his pen.

"I'm alive and happy to be so. I care more about that than the scar on my face." I realize my fingers betray me by tracing my raw scar, and I stuff my hand in my hoodie pocket.

"In and of itself, a belief in the paranormal does not mean someone is suffering from a mental illness. You did not disclose this in your assessment the last time you were here. You did not disclose much at all. But by your parents' reporting of the events they *do* know about, you have exhibited behavior consistent with someone who suffers from schizophrenia. Someone who believes in ghosts does not normally display such a marked difference in personality."

When I say nothing in response, the doctor forges on. I know from the hollow feeling in my stomach where this is going.

"Since you're a minor, your parents have the authority to medicate you for your own safety and for the safety of those around you. This decision has not been made lightly. Their highest priority is to see you well and adjusted. Able to live your life as close to normal as possible."

"Normal," I whisper, mostly to myself. "I'll never be *normal*."

I've been fighting medication because the night I cut my mother in the kitchen, the sedative made me feel weak, less concrete in my body. And because the phantom was still there even beneath the haze of the drug. She wants to climb inside me, claim me. I can feel it, like she's pounding on the door of my soul. What if, by taking the pills, I become too weak to fight her off? And somewhere, deep inside me, I think medication is poison. I don't know where that thought comes from, but it feels like a conviction. Now they want to force me to take it, and because I'm a minor, they say I have no choice.

"Ryan, this is not your fault, nor is it something you can will away. The bravest thing you can do is to come to a place of acceptance so you can move forward in life, healthier and better able to cope. You don't have to suffer."

You do. Yes, you do.

—

We fill my new head-med prescription, and after the first week of taking it, I don't feel much difference. My mom is worried that the prescription isn't effective. "Maybe that's because I'm not mentally ill?" I offer with some sarcasm.

My mom cries openly while driving home from my follow-up visit to Dr. Collier's. "I feel like I'm losing everyone I love. Your bodies stay here, but your minds become a room I can't enter. It's been a long road with your father's PTSD. He's having bad dreams again. Did you know that?" I didn't, but she doesn't wait for my answer. "Your grandma slips deeper into herself every day, and you . . . you've changed before my very eyes." She wipes her face with the sleeve of her flowered blouse.

"Why didn't Gran come with us to the doctor?" I ask in a feeble attempt to change the subject.

Mom notices and gives me a raised eyebrow. "She isn't feeling well. I couldn't rouse her this morning, so I let her stay in bed. She should be fine for this short while."

I think of Gran's hitchhiking adventure and how quickly she can slip away. She shouldn't be alone. "I lost her," I blurt. "After I got out of the hospital. She went hitchhiking for pancakes."

My mom's eyes pop open in alarm. "She went—" Then she laughs, but quickly stops herself with the back of her hand to her mouth. Her laugh isn't carbonated like before.

Now her laugh is flat soda: sweet but lifeless. The car speeds up, and after a few tense minutes she says, "You should have told me."

"I know. I'm sorry."

"We were always so close," she says. "I feel like I've lost my daughter."

"I'm sorry." I'm marinating in it.

"I know you didn't want to take the pills, but they brought your father back to me. If they bring you back, then it seems worth it."

I swallow the lump in my throat. The daughter she knew is gone. Visions of the girl they miss scroll through my head like a movie montage. Everyone's fighting to save the girl they love.

We're all losing the fight.

Suddenly I feel sick. There are kids whose parents don't fight to save them. The strange, potent thought comes from last night's dream, but with such emotional force, I'm pierced as if it's my own story. It's one of those visions, populated by people with dour, pale faces who are crowding in on me, laying hands on me, that I had to scribble about in my journal. The visions are increasing and uncontrollable. They're like nightmares while awake. *Daymares.*

"Have you ever dreamed people you don't know?" I ask, wanting to know if this is a normal thing. I dream the same cast of strangers so frequently, I feel like I'm starting to know them. And deeply hate them. Powerful emotions—hate, anger, despair—skip like stones on the lake of my dreams and visions, but otherwise, in day-to-day life, they sink to the bottom.

My mom gives me one of her assessing glances, full of concern. "I think we are all of the characters we dream. Different parts of our psyche playing various roles."

So does that mean I hate myself?

My dad phones and asks if my mom can come handle some paperwork for the exhibition jump for the facility visit of the organizers of the X Games. He's called in some favors and has arranged for more jump planes to be onsite when they come. The hangar is getting the top-to-bottom white-glove treatment. With each day, his anticipation ramps up. It has the faint trace of desperation.

My body hums with jittery excitement at going to the airport, and it's a welcome sensation, something new. Maybe if I skydive, I'll feel like myself again. The thought of jumping makes me queasy all of a sudden, but to be all the way alive, to experience something more than guilt and confusion, I have to do everything I can to be *that* girl—and that girl eats and breathes the drop zone.

—

The desert is particularly gorgeous today. The sky is so blue that the mountains look like they've been painted against it. I'm glad for the open space of the Mojave. I think I'd be overwhelmed in the bustling city with its colors and crowds and . . . glass.

My dad is in a good mood, or at least he looks like he is. When we walk in, he's prepping two full loads of jumpers — a good sign for business, but my parents exchange a glance that is a question about me and my follow-up visit with Dr. Collier. Even though I haven't wigged out in front of them in almost a week, he probably wants confirmation that the meds are permanently dousing the crazy in me.

Whether Dr. Collier realizes it or not, the way he speaks of schizophrenia and bipolar disorder has burdened me with a sense of hopelessness. The statistics don't support my notion of "getting over this someday." According to him, most people with schizophrenia never recover or live normally. I wondered why I even needed the medication when he said it often doesn't help with problems like craving isolation, feeling numb, or having no interest in life in general. What's the point, then?

My mom is talking to my dad about how we're busier because word has gotten out that we're being considered for the X Games. People want in on that action. The energy of the drop zone is a living thing, eddying around the bodies of the jumpers, infusing the air with an electric charge. I feel more alive. My blood pumps faster. This could be my medication.

Someone taps my shoulder. I startle.

Dom breaks into a chuckle. "I'm sorry, Ry. I didn't mean to scare you." He's wearing his jumpsuit and has a camera affixed to the top of his helmet. His dimples flash as he grins. He has a full-wattage smile.

"It's okay. I'm sorry I've been cold to you." My admission also startles me. Seeing him standing here, with cute dimples and sweet eyes, makes me feel warmth, and that's another novel sensation after days of feeling numb and disoriented. Scared.

Dom looks into me so deeply, I swear he can see every secret under my skin. I don't know if anyone has ever looked at me so penetratingly. But then I realize: *He has.* He's also trying not to say anything about my shaved hair, but his eyes can't help but flick to the top of my head. "I want to talk more with you, but I have to go up and film a jump," he says, regret in his rich voice. "Paco broke his ankle on a jump, and Kelsey's sick, so we're way short on camera crew. We need to get you back in the air. I'm worried we won't have someone to film the big-way. So can I talk to you when I land?"

"Okay."

I don't know what else to say, because there is too much to say. He was my other best friend. More than that . . . my first love. I don't know what we are now. I don't want to carelessly hurt him the way I've hurt Joe and my mother.

"We can talk later," I promise, and watch his brown eyes light up with hope. He sweeps in and kisses my cheek, then darts out toward an airplane waiting on the tarmac with its engine droning like a million bees.

My father clears his throat. "I've got a surprise for you," he says, pulling me outside through the wide-open hangar doors. He leads me onto the tarmac, where rows of parked planes wait to fly. People are gathered around one old plane in particular. It's enormous—gleaming polished metal with four engines and bubbles of glass on the nose and un-derbelly. A painted pinup girl smiles over her shoulder at us from the nose. "It's a B-17," he says through a wide grin.

He looks like a little boy on Christmas. I feel the most genuine smile erupt on my face. It pulls tight at my wound.

"How many girls do you know who get to ride in a real-live World War Two bomber?"

My smile fades. "Ride?" I ask, trying not to sound appre-hensive. "We get to go up in it?"

"You've been doing better, right? Besides, I'll be going up too. It'll be the ride of your life, kiddo. I've booked you a special seat." My dad leads me to the side of the plane, where stairs are propped against it, and gives me a leg up. He climbs in behind me. I feel like we've crawled into the belly of a metal whale. Exposed bulkheads dotted with rivets wrap around us as we scuttle through the plane on a wooden platform.

I look out the waist gunner's window and try to imagine what it must've been like for the crew during the war. My father introduces me to the two pilots and directs me toward the nose of the plane. "It's the nose turret," he explains. "This is where the gunner would sit and shoot at planes approaching from the front or crossing the path of the bomber. Sit down."

I saddle myself in the metal seat, and he buckles me in. "I think it'd be scary being so exposed," I say.

"Well," he says, climbing out of the turret, "you're gonna find out."

I grab his leg. "Wait! I'm going to sit *here* while we fly? While we take off and land?"

His glorious smile returns. "Fantastic, right?"

"*Right.*"

One engine starts, then two, three, and four. The plane vibrates with the collective power of them. It's like a racehorse at the gate, bursting with the desire to run. The plane moves forward, taxiing toward the run-up area. I can't believe they're letting me sit here as we move to takeoff position and the runway begins to roll faster and faster right underneath my feet.

A "whoop!" flies out of me as we leave earth. I can't help it. This exhilaration tastes way sweeter than the acid of pain. My heart is pounding, and I feel so alive. We pull higher into the sky, and I try to disregard the reality that I'm essentially hanging from the bottom of the plane in a glass bubble.

I'd feel better with a chute on.

Progress.

The bomber banks to the right, and we climb higher. Mountains sweep past the left side of my glass bubble. If I lean forward enough, I can see in every direction. I'm sitting in the middle of a clear ball at fourteen thousand feet. The immense desert stretches from here to forever.

I stare in awe at its vastness. There is nothing in the world so rigidly true to itself as the desert. If the brown canvas of the Mojave had a dominant characteristic, it would be strength. The landscape is strong, stubborn: beauty that insists on its right to life on its own terms. I can appreciate that.

The steep turn of the plane makes my stomach lurch. My reflection materializes on the glass, stares out the window. We are watching the desert roll beneath our feet. Hands pressed against the glass like we could touch the sky. Strange, though, that I'm seeing the *back* of my head. I struggle with the laws of reflections for a moment. Shouldn't I see my *face* looking back at me in the glass?

It's not until my reflection turns slowly, looks sadly over her shoulder, that my heart stutters, and I realize who it is.

NiNETEEN

I DON'T KNOW WHY this time is different, but it's like I can *feel* her ferocious sorrow and desperation with me in this dome of glass. It magnifies her, as if she's standing, three-dimensional, right in front of me. She moves toward me, menacing. Her mouth is set in a grim line. Her eyes intent as she draws closer. She reaches for me.

My trembling fingers fight to unlock my harness, but the clip won't budge. Panicked, I kick at the apparition of myself, but my feet flail uselessly in air.

This other me, Death disguised as me, advances like prowling smoke.

"What do you want?" I yell, but not as loud as I intend. Fear has choked off my voice.

I want—

"Hey, kiddo. Some view you've got up here."

Our heads both pivot to see my father leaning into the bubble. I look back to the spirit, whose eyes now see only him. Her mouth moves. She's trying to speak to him, but he can't hear, and when her attention is not on me, neither can I. She lunges for my dad, and I want to fling myself in front of him but am still strapped in the damn chair.

His eyes narrow at my reaching arms. "You okay? Maybe this wasn't such a good idea . . ."

"I, uh, I just wanted a hug." It's the first thing that came to mind, but I realize it's true. But asking Nolan for a hug is like asking him to give me the Medal of Honor. He might wish he could, but he doesn't have it to give.

He gives my shoulder a squeeze instead. "We'll be landing soon."

"Will you stay with me?" My eyes dart to where she was. Her sudden absence is as much of a shock as her appearance.

He squats down on the floor next to me. "You bet."

"No, wait. Don't. There's no seat belt."

He shrugs. "I'll be fine." His eyes squint with his reassuring grin. "We'll be fine." I feel better with him here. He seems to sense the electric charge in the air and keeps talking, to reassure one of us. "When you've spent half your life jumping out of the confines of an airplane, you tend not to be so concerned with whether you're strapped in at all times."

I slowly unclench my hands when I realize my nails are digging into my palms. "Why do you love it so much? This place? Skydiving? You're happier here than anywhere else."

Nolan chews his lip, gives my question serious consideration. "Some people jump because they're addicted to the adrenaline, to the high. You're like that." His eyes scan my face as if he's suddenly wondering if that's still true. Neither of us is sure. "But for me, it's not about the high. I've seen so much in the war and"—he casts his gaze downward and rubs his hands over his hair with a sigh—"*done* so much, I'm . . . My default is to be numb. Jumping is the only thing that makes me feel truly alive. Even though I've been close to death a few times, risking death now, *by choice,* makes me appreciate life more."

"For some people, waking up to another day makes them appreciate life. That's enough for them."

He pats my leg. "But not for people like us."

In all the memories I can access, I can't remember a time when he has said we were alike.

"I blame myself for the fight we had when you low-pulled. Hell, I blame myself for your stunt. I know my wild child. I denied you a shot to prove yourself, so you set out to do that." His nostrils flare. "I'm sorry."

"It's okay."

He shakes his head. "It's not. I realized something the day you kooked out on acid. I haven't been very good at, well . . . I think you were looking for my attention. Acting out."

I heard what you said! You never wanted a girl. You said you weren't made to father anything but boys!

This recollection hits me full force. How did the ghost know before I did that my father didn't want me? It's like the dreams that have plagued me, only with different players. The shrill voice in my head rails at him, but I feel nothing but confusion: scattered memories blow in the wind, and I don't know which are real. There's no actual emotion behind the specter's very emotional words ringing in my ears. My father and I are alike in this way. I'm numb too.

He never wanted me.

"You never wanted me."

His mouth hangs open like he's wishing an argument would leap from his tongue and refute what I've said, but nothing comes out.

Instead of staring at him, waiting for his reply, I find myself looking out of the glass bubble. It appears as though the earth is reaching up to us, but we're descending. I close my eyes as we drop, attempting to block out the world and to shut out the girl whose apparition sits in the enclosed space with her head on her knees. She looks so sad. There's a part of me that wishes he hadn't shown up right when he did. I can't believe I'm thinking this, but I want her to finish her sentence. I want to know what it is that she wants.

She haunts me, but I have to know what's haunting her. If I knew that, could I put her to rest?

TWENTY

THE B-17 ROLLS to a stop. When the engines cut, it's like I've never heard silence this loud before. I have, though. I've been to a place where there are no sounds and no pictures but the memories in my head. I clung to them like a life raft. The night of the LSD, I was in a place so silent, it hurt.

My father helps me unfasten the clip on my belt, and I follow him out to the door. The stairs are propped against the side of the plane. Dom waits for me.

"We a go?" my dad asks him, to which Dom gives a thumbs-up. Probably another load of jumpers. I can't decipher this man-speak, but I'm glad to see that my father isn't blistering mad at Dom anymore. The drop zone is Dom's life too. He and his brother have practically lived here since their mom died. Their dad, well, he didn't want his kids either. It'd kill Dom to lose this family.

For the second time, I get a rush of loss like a hot wind that's blown through me. This was *our* life, together. Then the air inside me stills.

My dad walks away but looks back at us as he does.

"How've you been?" Dom asks.

I bite my lip, force a smile. "Been better."

"That could be interpreted two ways."

"Probably should be."

Dom reaches up, smooths his hand over my newly cropped hair. Bumps of pleasure flare on my skin. "I never thought I'd say this, but you're even more badass without your hair. Gives you a rougher edge."

"I feel softer on the inside. I mean, not because of the hair, but because—"

His head cocks to the side. "I knew what you meant, babe."

I look down at my feet. He doesn't let me linger in awkwardness. His finger tilts my chin up. His stare is a cocoon. "You've been through a lot. An experience like you had, nearly dying, it can *change* people, change their whole outlook on life."

"That's what I've been trying to tell everyone. I *am* changed. I see life differently now: how fragile and *thin* this world is. People don't realize." I reach my hand out to the air and touch nothing but the open doorway between this life and the next. "It's right there. We can walk right through it. I'm scared to walk through it again, so I'm being extra careful. But it's like nobody wants me to change. They don't want this careful Ryan. They want me the way I was. I see how reckless I was before. How careless. I would think everyone would be happy I've changed from . . . *that*. But none of you are."

Dom's hand slides down my arm, and he gives my fingers a squeeze. "I'm not gonna lie and tell you that you made people feel comfortable. You've scared everyone you know at least once. Hell, you made my nuts shrivel up in fear with that low-pull jump." He smiles and kisses my fingers. His voice softens again. "Thing is, you reminded everyone that the walls of safety they put around themselves are complete bullshit. By living out loud and full-on, you're a reminder that they aren't fully living, that they are too afraid. Baby, you're a mirror for their fears."

Maybe I'm a mirror for my own fears.

My breath catches. Maybe the doctor was right. Maybe there are things about myself I don't want to see.

"Change scares people too," he says. "You seeming so different scares the stones out of them. But I believe in your fire. It's still in there, just not raging right now, and that's okay. Gives people a chance to catch their breath."

"Beautiful, the way you see me. The way you talk." He's like Gran that way.

Impossibly, Dom's smile grows even wider. "It's like you don't know me at all. Ah," he says, dropping my hand and pulling something from his pocket. "Which reminds me. I was going to wait until later, but now seems like the right time. Close your eyes and open your hand."

I grin and shut my eyes with my palm upturned, waiting. Whatever he places there is light: a little more weight than the warm air swirling around us. "Okay," he whispers.

There's an intricately folded origami tiger standing in the palm of my hand.

"I'm holding a tiger," I say.

"I used to say that about you."

"I know. I'm sorry."

"Nah. Don't be. I'm glad we're talking again, like we used to."

I turn the tiger over in my hand. He worked so hard on it, even painted it with minuscule strokes of color for the stripes and face.

"It's got a message for you," he says with a sly grin, but places his finger over my lips when I begin to ask what. "You'll discover the message when you're ready. Keep it somewhere safe. Now let's go back to the hangar."

He doesn't grab my hand or put his arm around me, which I'm grateful for. I'm happy to have had the quiet moment talking with him. He didn't make me feel bad for being different. Acceptance is a lovely thing when you know you don't belong.

I'm surprised to see the hangar doors closed when we approach. It's too early in the day to close. There were too many people around earlier to turn them away. This can't be good for business. Dom takes one side of the sliding metal door and heaves it open.

A single reckless white balloon escapes through the crack of the door and out into the daylight, floating up into the sky. Free.

I squint and watch it bob and soar on the currents until it becomes one with the sky, disappearing from view.

"Surprise!"

Music kicks in, people are blowing on kazoos, and the hangar is filled with balloons and streamers and people with happy faces. I look to Dom. "Happy birthday!" they all yell.

"It's . . . it's your birthday?"

With a perplexed tilt of his head he replies, "It's *your* birthday."

I don't know what to say. My parents walk toward me with satisfied grins that they pulled off the surprise.

"You didn't remember your own birthday?" my mom says with a hearty hug and a laugh that doesn't cover the consternation in her eyes. Her brows cinch. "That's something coming from the girl who surprised *us* last year by throwing her own surprise party."

My grandmother is perched in a lawn chair in the middle of the hangar, smoking a Swisher Sweet cigar. My mom lied about her being home alone. Fatigue draws at the wrinkled skin around Gran's mouth, but she's smiling and nodding her head to the music. Apparently, her not feeling well was all a ruse.

Avery leans against the wall under the flags in the back of the hangar. Her eyes find Dom before they turn to me, and then she smiles big and waves. I frown, not trusting a smile that looks like an afterthought.

Numerous skydiving friends and friends from school approach to wish me happy birthday. Too many faces and names compete for space. Too many jumbled memories. My eyes scan the room for a familiar comfort to anchor me. Joe's absence is a hole in my chest.

I have random conversations with friends who feel like strangers. Some have red cups of I-don't-even-know-what sloshing around inside. Word has obviously gotten around about my incident with the LSD, because people safely stick to benign topics like their jobs, what they've been doing over summer vacation, and how bad they don't want school to start again. Their mouths are moving and smiling, but their eyes are asking if I'm okay.

More than once, I catch people staring at the pink slash across my brown cheek.

"Attention!" The sergeant has everyone's eyes on him with that one word through the megaphone. "I've got a couple of announcements to make." The music volume decreases. "For anyone who's doing tomorrow's Sierra Golf demo jump, take it easy tonight." There's a chorus of good-natured mumblings and laughter. My dad quiets them with one raised hand. "The weather's spotty, but it looks like we're still a go. And I know you've all been anxious for news about the big-way. It'll be next weekend. Practice jumps have been ongoing and will continue tomorrow after the demo jump. Even if you are not participating in the big-way, come out and show support. The larger the crowd, the better we look, and I'm pretty sure you'd like them to pick us for the X Games."

Everyone cheers. Out of the corner of my eye, I see Avery and Dom having an intense discussion by the bathrooms. He turns to walk away, but she fists his T-shirt and tugs him back toward her. The rage that shakes my body is enough for two people. I know I've been confused and conflicted, but no one likes to be easy to replace. And what kind of cousin moves in at all, let alone so quickly? Her pout makes me wonder what's gone on between them.

Dom looks up and catches me watching them. I spin around and head out the door to the lawn area. I want to be alone, but there are a few people out here ignoring the approaching summer storm, which has turned the sky over the mountains from blue to gray. It's still sunny overhead, though. A few people are swimming in the pool, partying on the lawn, and playing Frisbee. The wind kicks up, lifting the orange Frisbee and tossing it aside.

Dom calls my name. I don't want to talk to him. I'm chaotic. She is screaming inside my head once more, and I can't take it. I hear my name called again. I hear his name in my own head. I feel trapped from without and within.

There's a hand on my shoulder that I know is Dom's. I dive away from him into the sun-warmed water. Air bubbles tickle my bare scalp and skin. Muffled voices and the warble of water fill my ears. I wish I could stay under forever. I look up at the magnified feet dangling into the water, but then they rise up and disappear. I'm blissfully alone in a cocoon of peace.

A big splash sends the water shifting. I turn. Dom swims toward me underwater, his black hair undulating like burned grass in wind. His dark eyes are fixed on me. A memory flashes from the night in the trailer when his hair looked like waves, then flashes to our kissing in the mirror. I shove the memory away.

I push up from the scratchy bottom of the pool and kick upward, but Dom's anticipated that, and we bob to the surface at the same time, just inches apart. "This is a fun game," he pants. His face is anything but amused.

"I don't want to talk."

Hear me! she screams within me.

His eyes squint in confusion. "You just said you don't want to talk."

"That wasn't me!" I clamp my hand over my mouth. I can't believe I spoke her words. I'm possessed. She's controlled me, and I'm terrified and mortified. My body trembles so hard with fear that my teeth chatter and my head shakes. I'm out of control.

Dom's eyes narrow. Drops of water glisten on his brown shoulders, and I look away, try to focus on the glaring yellow T-shirt he dropped on the concrete. Too soon, my gaze falls back on him.

"If this is about that conversation you saw with Avery, you got the wrong idea."

"You don't know what my ideas are. You don't know what's in my head. I said I don't want to talk to you right now."

He slaps the water with his hand. "Then what the hell do you want?"

We stare at each other, waiting, challenging. It's a dance I have many memories of, and it usually ended in . . . makeup sex. My heart picks up speed like it has its own mind. Will my body ever belong to me?

I watch the water drip from the points of his wet eyelashes and, beneath them, clouds reflect in the depths of his eyes. His lips are wet, slightly open. He's waiting with suffering eyes for me to tell him what I want.

He's waiting for me to tell him it's still him.

Thunder rolls over the mountains and through me.

"Tell me," Dom says, his voice quivering, "that you're still my girl." His fingers tighten on the ridge of muscle at the small of my back.

"Why? So you can run to Avery if I'm not?"

He doesn't answer. Doesn't move or even blink. He doesn't even look like he can breathe until I answer him.

"B-But," I stutter, the truth fighting a tug of war within me, "I — I'm not the same girl."

"I'm still yours, Ryan. Always. That's not gonna change no matter how much you do. I love you."

I start to reply, but he swoops his arm around my waist and pulls me against his body. Bubbles rush up my sides and back, delighting my skin. My hands find their way to the slant where his collarbone meets his smooth chest. Part of me wants to push away. Part of me wants to feel the escalation of sensations: my blood pounding thicker through my body, my heart dancing against my ribs, this thirst I didn't even know I had.

Dom's other hand wraps behind my neck, and he pulls our heads together. His lips on mine feel like the crush of ripe summer berries, his tongue like wet velvet as we taste each other. Any resistance in my body has slipped away. Our breaths merge, mingling particles of ourselves. This kiss is a linking of some vital, beautiful essence of each of us. I melt into his cool skin, forgetting where I end and he begins.

Familiar yet foreign, this kiss is like a first kiss.

And a last.

"Ryan."

Nolan's voice. I don't have to look up to know he's staring at us with displeasure glinting in his eyes. Dom and I have an entire silent conversation before we turn to look at my father.

"Gran's not feeling well. We need to take her home now." I notice my dad's words are a bit slurred. This can't be good.

It's cold where my body separates from Dom's. I kick

through the water and pull myself out of the pool. I'll have to drive home like this. My dad doesn't seem to think it's odd that I jumped into the pool with all my clothes on. In fact, as far as they're all concerned, it's probably the most normal, spontaneously *Ryan* thing I've done since before the LSD trip.

"Let me go to the bathroom real quick and squeeze the water out of my clothes?"

My dad nods. "Okay, but make it quick. Your mom wants to get your grandma home ASAP." Dom sloshes out of the pool, and my dad says to him, "Watch things for me here, would you? I'm going in case the girls need my help with Gran. I'll be back in a bit to close up and get things ready for the demo jump."

"Yes, sir." Dom nods. "Hope Gran feels better," he says to me.

My sneakers squeak as I jog past the rows of rental jumpsuits and helmets hanging on a rack in the hallway on the way to the women's bathroom. Following an inexplicable impulse, I look over my shoulder to see if anyone's watching me, then grab someone's stray duffel bag and stuff a jump helmet, goggles, and a black jumpsuit inside.

I skid to a guilty halt in the bathroom. Avery is applying lipstick in the mirror and glances through it at me. I tuck the duffel against my belly and go into a shower stall to remove my sopping clothes, wringing them out as much as I can before slipping them back on.

"So." Avery's voice is higher pitched than normal. "Things are back on with you and Dom, huh? That's great." She's sitting on the sink counter when I come out.

"I'm so glad I have you, *cousin,* to keep an eye on the people who are trying to *comfort* him." The words are out before I can think to push them away. I *was* ready to let him go. I think . . . I don't know. But I do know the world is made up of circles of people, and in most circles, it's totally uncool for other girls in yours to pick up on the guy you were with.

"Is this all an act?" Avery asks, her blue eyes accusatory. "I mean, sure, you were always more flamboyant than everyone else. But I knew it was just to get attention. You could be doing that now, for all anyone knows, planting your flag on cray-cray mountain so we'll all look at you."

I want to hit her so badly, my fisted hands ache. "And what about you?" I ask. "You think hanging around exceptional people makes you exceptional?"

"Yeah, well, I don't need to be exceptionally screwed up just to get noticed. What's the matter? Afraid if you act normal, you'll be invisible?"

TWENTY-ONE

Gran doesn't look very well. There's a grayish cast to her wrinkled skin, like it's been wrung of its color the way I wrung the pool water from my clothes. I squeeze her hand as we drive home.

"I feel as wispy as those clouds out there," she says.

"How did you know it was cloudy?"

"I can smell them." She yawns like a sleepy toddler. "And the quality of the light. It's not as bright on my skin."

I love the way she talks. I'm struck with a panicked sadness. I don't want to lose her gentleness and wisdom. I don't want to think of her in a dark place. But then, maybe that only happens to some people. People like me.

"I feel like I should pray."

"But you've never prayed," she tells me over another yawn. Through the rearview mirror, my father squints his eyes at me, and my mother begins biting her nails but doesn't look back.

"Yes — yes, I pray." Maybe it's Gran's dementia. She has to be wrong. There've been prayers. I've drowned in prayers. Though I can't conjure a specific memory of doing it alone or with them. Only an inner knowing that my knees have been worn red from praying, praying so hard for something that my soul ached with the void of not getting it. "I've been angry at God."

This time my mom does whip her head sideways, and she pierces me with a black look. Unease creeps through me. I've said something wrong. Still, I can't help but stubbornly think that maybe if I pray for Gran, she'll feel the brightness of heaven on her skin. Gran pats my hand like she knows I'm thinking blue thoughts. She probably does. I'm sweating anger and emanating bitterness from my fight with Avery.

"Avery accused me of faking everything," I whisper to Gran. "For attention."

"Psht. Don't think on her and her sour words. Treat the bad ones like the vinegar they rolled in and the sweet ones like they were dipped in honey."

Once home, everyone works together to get Gran into the house and to her room. She seems more disoriented than usual and keeps asking me to sing for her again. My mom and I share confused looks as we help Gran into nightclothes and get her into bed.

"She doesn't want dinner." My mom sighs as she shuts Gran's bedroom door. "That's not a good sign."

Her attention is soon diverted to my dad, who rummages loudly in the kitchen, pulling a snack from the fridge. His car keys jangle in his pocket. My mother insisted on driving us home from the drop zone. Her eyes narrow as he walks toward the door.

"You don't really need to go back, do you?" she asks. "Dom said he'll keep an eye on things."

He glances my way.

She grabs his hand. "Please, no more to drink tonight, Nolan."

He sucks the inside of his cheek with a defiant look and says, "I'll see you later." And he's gone.

Later, as soon as I'm sure my mom is asleep, I pull the jump helmet from the bag and sit on my desk with two rolls of decorative duct tape. Dom's origami tiger stares at me from the black surface of the desk. What is the tiger's message? I've been thinking about it and have an idea. The conversation with my father in the B-17 sparked it. *Jumping is the thing that makes me feel truly alive.* My father and I are alike. It's true for him. Once upon a time, it was true for me.

When I wake in the predawn, I smile at the helmet, a darn good representation of a tiger head if I do say so myself. I worked on it nearly all night. It's not inconspicuous, but it's not the recognizable Red Baron, either. I stuff it in my bag and jog down to catch my dad, hoping he hasn't already left. A dented pillow and tousled blanket lie on the couch.

I find him leaning on his forearms at the new kitchen table, wooden this time. When he looks up at me, I see the dark circles that rim his eyes, and his hair looks darker because it's greasy. He's wearing the same clothes from yesterday.

"You okay?"

One huge swig of coffee later, he nods. "Affirmative. What're you doing up so early?"

Forcing my feet not to shuffle, I say, "I enjoyed being at the DZ yesterday."

"So you were surprised?"

"You have no idea. I was wondering if I can go again today? Just to hang around, maybe help if I can?"

There's an awkward beat of silence before he shrugs and answers. "You take your meds?"

I nod.

"Sure."

On the way there, my dad turns his head away from me when he yawns. He needn't try to hide it. I'm yawning too. The car drifts over the center line of the highway. He casually corrects course, then ducks his head to look up through the windshield. Bulbous gray clouds obscure the sky, making it look as if we're trapped underneath the tops of jellyfish in a vast ocean. Scattered raindrops patter on the windshield.

No one else has arrived yet. The hangar looks cold and shuttered. Because of the chill of the morning, we enter through a side door and leave the main doors closed. It takes my eyes a moment to register that some of the lumps on the packing pads are actually people curled up in sleeping bags. The place is an after-party disaster. Red plastic cups and wrinkled balloons litter the countertops. Someone's bra is strewn over a picture of the Golden Knights, the Army skydiving team. The place smells like old nacho cheese and dirty feet.

"Get on that. Christ, it's like having twenty goddamn kids." While my father gets to the business of readying for the demo jump, I busy myself with cleanup, tossing cups into a large black trash bag and wiping the check-in counter clean. Yvon, one of our pilots, shows up. She has a slight limp—I've no idea why she limps, but feel like I should know. She also has pretty caramel hair that sparks with silver threads when the light hits it just right.

As I'm pondering why my memory is like the shallow end of an ocean, she elbows me in the side. "Glad to see you here, little miss." Yvon has the ready smile of someone who knows that no matter what steaming pile of crap life hands you, you can always mold it into something better than what it was. She doesn't say these things with words, but I see it in her eyes. She's been around and back around. "Place isn't the same without you."

"I'm not the same without it."

She nods. "Roger that." She pulls a hair tie off her wrist and tugs her hair into a ponytail before pulling it through the back of a baseball cap. "When do you suppose you'll get back up there?"

I like that it's *when* and not *if*. She's more sure of the idea than I am.

"Soon." I don't know why, but I find myself telling her the truth: Yesterday, after talking to my dad in the B-17 and after interpreting the message from Dom's origami tiger, I had an epiphany. "I need to get back in the air soon. It's the only way to really live."

One side of her mouth lifts into a smile, and she limps away to go fuel and preflight the plane for the golf-course demo. Jumpers begin to arrive, disheveled in that roll-out-of-bed-and-roll-out-of-an-airplane, it's-just-another-Saturday kind of way. But they're excited. Everyone loves jumping into a new location, and the golf-course grass is a luxurious change from the scrubby desert sand.

Soon my dad is too busy checking people in on the manifest, answering questions, and going over the flight plan with Yvon to notice me sneaking into the restroom with my duffel bag. My heart pounds against my ribs as I slip my legs into the black jumpsuit. I shouldn't be this nervous, but I am. Doubts settle on me. Maybe I interpreted the tiger's message wrong. I don't know if I can do this. Hundreds of jumps mean nothing when they feel like they were performed by someone else.

The jumpsuit is too small for my height, and I curse myself for picking the wrong size off the women's rental rack. I'm Catwoman with a tiger's head. Hiding in a toilet stall in the bathroom until right before the hop is the only way I can think of to stay concealed. Goggles and gloves help, but an extra body in the jump plane is going to be hard to hide. For the hundredth time, I remind myself that this is who I am. I need to do this. I cannot go from being fearless to fearful. It's alienating me, making everyone question the differences between the old me and the new me — and my seeing the eyes has made them question my very sanity. Most of all, though, it's making me feel like I'm less than what I was.

I can't believe that Avery accused me of faking. She's full of crap, but she got one thing right: I'm standing out for things opposite from what made me stand out before. I'm standing out because I'm acting like the walking dead.

My hands are shaking when I check the time. The demo jumpers are to board the plane in five minutes. I take deep breaths as I slide my legs through the leg straps, heft the parachute pack onto my back, and slide my arms through the harness before buckling it to my chest.

There is a tiny gold angel pin on the nylon chest strap. I finger it before sliding the helmet over my head. I've got nearly three hundred jumps under my belt. I can do this. So why do I feel like I'm about to walk to the electric chair? Trembling, I steel my resolve and force my legs to move.

It's go time.

Outside, the wind kicks up the smell of wet sagebrush and moist earth. The windsock complains, shaking its fist at the eastern sky. Engines are already humming. Jumpers file out of the hangar in a disorderly procession — demo team and solo jumpers mixed together. The lack of organization is good for me. I'm just another bird in the flock.

I slip into the troop without anyone taking much notice except to gawk at my body in the skintight suit. Trying to catch my breath isn't easy as the engines push wind into our faces. We wait under the wings for our turn to board. When it's mine, I heft myself up through the jump door. With the thrust of the engines, the metal vibrates under my hands, sweaty in the gloves. A hand reaches out and pulls me up. I suck in my breath when Dom and I lock eyes.

The astonishment on his face quickly fades. His brows crinkle in confusion, and he chews a moment on his lip. That's the evidence of the war within him: whether to say anything about the fact that I'm suited up and ready for action.

"Nice helmet," he finally says, and nods me toward the back of the plane.

I make my way to the metal wall behind the pilots and scrunch into a ball. I'm not sure I can go through with this . . . When my father spoke of how alive skydiving makes him feel, when he spoke of how similar we are, I wanted nothing more than to feel both those things in my body instead of the unvarying static of detachment. I wanted to feel the muscle memory of being me, not just see me in the pictures in my head.

I am Ryan Poitier Sharpe.

I am bold and fearless.

I show people how to live life to the fullest. Pushing limits is in my blood, right?

So why am I so terrified? Why are my heels tapping a strange song on the floor of the plane? I need to relax, trust myself. My body is humming, but I can't tell if it's pure fear or the ghost of me inside, longing to fly free again.

I can do this.

I must do this.

It will prove to everyone who I am. That I'm back.

It will prove to me . . .

. . . the only thing that matters—I am alive.

Everyone is seated in two long rows. I'm glad to be in the very back of one, so that my trembling might only be felt by the person in front of me. I keep my eyes closed for the eternity it takes us to climb to fourteen thousand feet.

Someone has opened the jump door. The engines throttle back. The plane lurches a bit in the wind.

Burbles of laughter erupt from me as we dip and sway, and a few people gasp.

The guy in front of me turns around. "What could be funny?"

I don't know. It's all funny. It's terrifying and hilarious.

I don't answer him. He's looking at me like I'm crazy.

"Only thing funny is the boss's brain," he says. "Bright idea, going ahead with this weather."

"You didn't have to get on the plane!" I yell over the noise.

Dom is suddenly standing over me. "Neither did you. Stand up."

As if on cue, everyone stands and begins checking each other's equipment.

"Slow is fast," I hear a girl next to me mumble as she fixes something on her rig. Dom moves behind me to perform the same checks on my gear. "If this means you're coming back to yourself, then I'll trust you," he says against my ear. I turn my face toward him.

"How did you know it was me?"

He rolls his eyes and grins. "I know this body." His fingers cling possessively to my hips. He taps on my newly painted helmet. "But the tiger gave you away."

Heat warms my cheeks. Despite all our times together, Dom feels like a stranger to me. His familiarity with my body is unnerving but scintillating, too.

"Let the demo team and other jumpers go first, and then go out right after them, okay?"

I nod, swallowing down my fear, but the plane pitches to

the right and terror courses through me again. I realize I'm clutching Dom's hand. He kisses my cheek. "You got this. Have fun, tiger." He heads to the doorway.

Everyone but me is huddled in a pack near the open jump door. They need to go out in a group to be able to track to one another in the air and get into formation. Spatters of rain have made the doorway slippery with wetness. Yvon continues in slow flight, and Dom calls out a count. Our eyes meet, and I see the barest hint of a smile.

The plane does a sudden drop in the increasing wind from the storm. I was slowly moving toward the doorway, but that drop stops me. Lightning cracks outside the window. In its spectral glow, her face looks in on me.

"Go!" Dom yells to the team over the wind.

Bodies fly out the door, and my own body is pulsing with admiration and fear. With every beat of my heart, I hear her voice.

Death whispers, *Go, go, go.*

She's challenging me.

I take another step, but as the last of the team hurls itself out of the opening, the plane lurches again. Dom is supposed to jump with them, but he's still in the plane and staring at me with an anxious look on his face. I hear an incessant buzzing sound from the front of the aircraft as the tail dips lower. "Goddamn it!" Yvon yells. "Stall warning! Get out! Get out!"

Terror pushes me flat against the wall. Opposite me, rain coats the windows with rivulets, and another crack of lightning illuminates the sky outside the plane. In that eerie light, her face stares at me.

"Get out!" Yvon yells again.

I shake my head. I'll stay in the plane. No way am I jumping into the rain and lightning, right into *her* arms.

Strong hands vise my biceps, and before I can protest, before I know what's happened, Dom forcibly throws me out of the airplane into the rain.

TWENTY-TWO

MY BODY TRIES to curl in on itself. I remember being in freefall once and wondering if I wasn't real. If I could be someone else's dream. I want someone to wake up now, to make this nightmare end, but a lucid alarm within me trills and forces me to open my eyes. Needles of rain hit my lips and chin. I am falling so fast, it's as though it's raining *up* into my face. My right arm jerks, and I realize Dom has tracked to me and has hold of one of the grips on my jumpsuit. We are plummeting together toward the ground. He holds his free hand out and gives me a hand signal. His fingers are spread and his palm is in a flat position.

I don't understand. Panic is a blindfold. Panic is mind bleach. Panic has frozen me.

But then my mind snaps back into what I know.

I uncurl my arms and legs and flatten my body, but I'm

buffeting and rocking as if I'm on my stomach on a water-bed. Nothing is going as planned. I'm stiff with terror and, more than that, disbelief that I'm not in Death's hands but in Dom's.

This is all her doing. She's after me. Maybe it wasn't my own mind convincing me to jump but her evil whisperings. I glance at Dom's intense face. Because of me she could get a two-for-one deal.

I need him to let go of me. I can't be responsible for his death.

When I attempt to pull my arm free of his grasp, he grits his jaw into a rigid mask and grabs for my upper leg. His helmet crashes into my ribs. The world tilts and rotates violently. I feel like I'm rising up as Dom plummets below me. My upper body jerks upright, pulling my spine straight, knocking a grunt out of me. My legs sweep underneath me, swinging forward past my chest before gravity pulls them toward the ground.

Dom has pulled my chute.

The parachute snaps in the wind over my head. My goggles fog up, blinding me to the wet desert below. I can't see him. The thought comes to me that I've never been so alone. But that's not true. I've been the kind of alone that you think you'll never come back from.

Yet I came back.

Turbulence throws me into a sudden drop and startles me into action. I have only one job right now, and that's to land without killing myself. I reach up the risers and clasp the toggles, freeing them, and try to maneuver toward the large patch of green in the desert that must be the golf course the demo team jumped for. Soon I realize there's no way I'm going to reach it. All I can do is stay stable and calm despite my racing heart, dry throat, and shaking limbs.

Sagebrush and cacti are splashed haphazardly all over the flat canvas of desert. This isn't like landing at the DZ, where there's an enormous circle wiped clean. It's like landing in a minefield. Rain coats my goggles, making it difficult to see, and I'm too scared to let go of the toggles to wipe them. It wouldn't matter anyway; they'd just be coated with water again within seconds.

The closer I get to the ground, the faster my descent feels, like the earth is pushing up to meet me hard and fast. The wind kicks me around, and I'm too afraid to turn or do anything but keep myself straight as possible as I drop. Brush catches my legs right before impact, and I hit face-down, rolling over and over. It's like rolling on boulders of cut glass. My legs sting, my cheeks burn, and I've got scrapes under my chin.

Mercifully, I roll to a stop. I'm wound like a burrito

in my parachute. Rain pelts down on it so that the nylon fabric clings to my face. I will be smothered. Fighting and clawing at the chute, I wiggle one hand free and unclasp the helmet, rip the goggles off my face, and gasp for air against the material. I'm so bound in the chute and lines that I'm hogtied on the desert floor.

There's laughter in my head. *Laughter.* I want to cry through her amusement.

Crazy is starting to look more and more plausible.

Burned-red anger spreads like fire from my belly through my body. I don't want to hear her now. Never again. She has become my tormentor. This moment should have been my victory for booming back into life, my triumph for being bold and fearless, and I'm being laughed at for crash landing. I'm humiliated by a spook.

I flail and struggle to free myself. Will I be stuck here like this? Will someone eventually find me, mummified in my own parachute among the Joshua trees and sagebrush, eyes staring at heaven?

My name. I hear my name. And footsteps in the dirt. Hands touch my cheeks through the fabric. "Are you okay?" Dom's breathless voice asks. I croak out a yes. "Don't move," he says, kneeling over my legs. I hear a metallic click. "Not . . . one . . . move . . ." he warns as he puckers a wad of the chute above my face, creating a tent over my nose, and then the glint of a knife slashes through the fabric from my nose to my navel.

Cool air and rain hit my skin, and Dom pulls me to sitting, shaking me. "What the hell happened?"

"You—you threw me out. I could have died. Do you want me to die?" At once I'm filled with such certainty that he did want that. I don't know where this is coming from, but I *know* I've been at this fork in the road before, facing someone who didn't care if I died. There's a memory, or a dream, faded like an old photograph, of me asking that question before, and the answer was yes. It's too painful to be expendable. I can't look at his face.

Dom won't let me hide. He squeezes my cheeks until I'm facing him again. "You think I wanted you to die?" Incredulousness rips his voice into splinters. "I was trying to save you, Ryan! Yvon was fighting with a stalling plane. That's nowhere you want to be. You fucking froze up there. I've never seen you like that, like everything you knew was wiped from your goddamn head!" Tears fill his eyes. His voice descends into a whisper, like he knows I'm in a deep, dark cave where it's only safe to reach me through whispers. "What's happened to you?"

"I don't know. The plane was jerking around, the rain . . . I saw . . . I think I hallucinated. I was scared."

He shakes his head, casting drops of water from the ends of his black hair. "Hallucinated? So what Joe told me is true? What Avery said wasn't lies?"

I can only imagine Avery's version of events of that night in the kitchen with the knife. But Joe? "Joe talked to you about me? When? Why?"

"He wanted to know if you'd said anything strange to me before the LSD. He was worried about you. He told me that he came to me because he knew that, besides your parents, I'm the only other person who wants what he wants: for you to be okay. I don't know what happened between you two, but Joe said he was done with you for now. Needed time away. He said I had to do everything I could to help you."

"Joe said that?"

"He threatened me, actually. I think it was the start of a friendship."

I want to explain, but I've been trying to explain to myself—and in my journals—what happened to me. I feel like I split in two. Nothing makes sense. "That night in the trailer—"

"No. I know what happened that night in the trailer. What happened to *you*? Where'd the Ryan go who was fearless, brave, so bright with life that she was all I could see? You saved me after my mom died, but you won't let me save you. I feel like I've lost my family all over again. It's like you died."

"I *did* die, Dom!"

"How can you say that? The doctors never did. You had a bad trip, and I hate that I had something to do with that, but ever since, you've been someone else."

"I know what I know. I died! I went someplace else. It was dark there. Now I'm back. Changed. I'm never gonna be that girl again! I'm trying and it's not . . . I came back as . . . this! Only nobody wants this! All of you loved someone else."

"You're wrong about that. *I* want you. I've never stopped loving you, but you've done nothing but turn your back on me, on us. Losing my mom was the worst pain, Ryan. You know that! But losing you because you're choosing it" — he pounds his fist on his chest — "it's killing me."

"Why do you think I jumped? I wanted to *feel!* I may be alive, but I don't feel things anymore. I've gone numb to everything but fear. I want to feel and I . . . I can't. You don't know what that's like, to feel *nothing good*."

The fear of a little boy, the desperation of a drowning man, the starvation — all these emotions rage in Dom's eyes. His grip on my cheeks softens. His thumb runs over my wet lips, and his eyes trace the lines like he's memorizing them. He presses his rain-drenched lips over mine.

I tense with surprise, my hands in fists at my sides, but

when he pulls me to his body, my palms find their way to the ridges of his chest. I may not be able to reach my frozen heart beneath the ice, but I can feel his heart crackling with fire under his soaked shirt as he clasps the back of my neck with one hand and runs his other down the small of my back.

"Do you feel this?" he asks, breathy against my mouth. My lips open to his, and his soft tongue meets mine. His mouth is so warm, I'm drawn to it. I can't stop from immersing myself. This time, when the world tilts, I don't notice it until the earth is against my back.

He covers my body with the length of his. I'm surprised by the fit of us. We fit together like a puzzle, a beautiful picture I saw long ago. His mouth trails heat down my neck. My fingers wind in the silky wetness of his hair as his tongue paints designs on my collarbone. He unzips my jumpsuit and rolls his fingers under the tank top I'm wearing. A moan of pleasure escapes his lips as he touches my skin. His hungry touch is the most exquisite sensation. Each gust of his fast breathing sends waves of heat spreading through my body, like he's blowing on kindling, waiting for it to catch.

A faint thawing warms my center. He found a way to reach through the ice.

Back arching up to meet him, mouth opening to be

devoured again and again, legs inching apart, straining against the confines of the parachute to encircle his waist, my body screams its remembrance of us, its remembrance of our love.

But there is one scream that's louder than my body.

No! You can't have him!

A sharp pain strikes my head, and Dom pulls away from me at the same time, startled. His face is flushed, but a stricken look pinches his brows together, leaves his beautiful mouth open in astonishment.

"You hit me?"

"What? No . . ." I swallow but can't push the truth under the current. It bobs to the surface. "*She* did."

You will not win! she cries. *You don't deserve this. You cannot love him. You cannot love him.*

I cover my ears. "I can't love you. I can't love you."

Dom shoves off me and stands. Black clouds halo his head as he looks down on me, lying on a blanket of nylon with soft rain dropping on my exposed skin. He holds his hands up in supplication. "Who's the chickenshit now, Ryan?"

No response comes from me, because if I open my mouth, her words will pour out again.

"You always said your dad was afraid to love, but it's you! You're afraid!" He's crying openly as he gazes at the desert, then back down at me. The agony in his eyes stabs at the ice inside me. How can I comfort him when I'm the reason he's in such pain? I'm the reason for Joe's pain, for my parents' pain and fear, and I'm the reason this poet and artist, this angel of a guy with his heart in his eyes, is ripping that heart out as he tears his gaze from me and turns away.

"I'm worth loving, you know," he tells me over his shoulder as I watch him leave me.

I sit there in stunned silence, the ice taking over. *Everyone's worth loving,* I think. *Everyone except me.*

TWENTY-THREE

THE DZ BUS rumbles down the mud-pocked road. We are all sticky with muggy dampness and humiliation. My father stands in the aisle at the front of the bus, steadying himself by holding on to the metal racks above our heads where our rigs are stored. Large circles of sweat dampen his pits. I can smell him. Fermented.

"What the hell happened out there?"

No one answers. Apparently, mine wasn't the only failed jump of the day. The team couldn't hook up in formation. The wind completely screwed with the spotting to the target landing zone at the golf course. Not that many spectators were there, anyway, with the weather. And half our people landed, like me, in the mud and sagebrush and had to trek around to find the golf course. It was a failure in every sense. Well, no one bounced.

"Thank your stars that wasn't the big-way. They'd laugh us out of the X Games!" Dad steps up to me, sitting alone on a bench near the front. Dom hasn't looked at me since I followed silently behind him to the golf course. Everyone else is strangely quiet, avoiding me. "And you!" he says, pointing his finger in my face. "What in the holy hell were you doing up there? Did you screw up my demo? Huh?"

It takes monumental effort to hold my chin up, but I do. "I thought I was ready—"

"Did you, now?" he sneers. "Last time I checked, I owned this drop zone, and I didn't clear your crazy ass to jump!"

His words are a slap that knocks my proud chin to the side. He called me out in front of everyone. He confirmed my insanity to the whole group. I'm trying to look out the window, but I can't, because instead of sagebrush rolling by, I'm haunted by the reflection in the glass. I curl forward on myself, resting my head on my knees.

"Sir!" It's Dom's voice. "It wasn't Ryan. It was—"

"Drunk." Someone coughs the word into their hand and a few snickers erupt. They're not blaming me. They're calling my dad out for the decision to jump in the storm.

I know why he did it. We need the money. Badly.

"Stop the bus!" my dad yells. Paco looks in the rearview mirror, shakes his head, and pulls the bus to a halt in the middle of the two-lane highway. "Two things are going to happen," Nolan says to the crowd. "The person who questions my decision is going to get their ass off this bus right now. This isn't the Army. I never had a choice when I was ordered to jump. I never got to squawk off about where we were jumping or what we had to do when we touched down. I never had a choice about who we attacked, or . . . who I killed! You think it was a choice to watch women die? Or children? My best friend?"

I'm so shocked, I can't breathe. I think the whole bus is holding its breath.

My dad draws a ragged inhale, trying to collect himself. He sways a bit on his feet. "*You* have a *choice* whether or not to get on that plane! Everyone has a choice! And the next person who wants to pipe off can meet me outside."

There is total silence. I'm not sure if anyone's ever seen him this enraged. Though, if I reach back in memory, I have. It's terrifying. Nolan holds up his hands in a cocky gesture that makes me wonder if he's drunk right now. Does he really want to fight? "No one?" he challenges. "That's what I thought."

But then the doors to the bus swing open. Everyone's eyes widen in wary surprise as Paco climbs out of the driver's seat, salutes my dad with his middle finger, and hobbles in his ankle brace out the open doors and down the highway in the pouring rain. We've lost one of our best jumpmasters, our best cameraman, and our driver.

Worse, seeing my dad's right-hand man abandon him has made everyone on this bus lose their confidence in Nolan Sharpe.

I stand, and my father pushes me back into my seat.

"Hey!" Dom yells. "Unacceptable, man."

I stand again, and my father glares with an unmasked warning. I brush past him and climb into the driver's seat of the bus, close the door, and pull away. Incredibly, no one stops me. They may doubt my sanity, but they don't doubt that I'm probably the only person who's driven this bus more than anyone else besides Paco, my father, and maybe Dom. I need to get the wheels rolling to a familiar place before we veer off into somewhere that's so far gone that we can't recover from it.

I may not be clear about a lot of things, but I'm clear that my father is teetering on his own edge and my family is on the verge of losing everything.

No one speaks for the rest of the drive. I think the worst of it is over, but when we arrive back at the skydive center, Yvon gravely informs my dad that there is major damage to the plane. It will take thousands of dollars and time that we don't have. The big-way is in one week.

Defeat is written all over my father's face as he shuts himself in his office with a bottle of Jack.

TWENTY-FOUR

"TAKE ME FOR A DRIVE," Gran demands.

She's leaning a bit too heavily on the back of a kitchen chair, and I'm edgy that it's going to tip over and spill her on the floor with it. I'm slanting off my seat, ready to jump for her. My mother rolls her eyes and swipes her brow with a flour-covered hand. She's baking: a sure sign of discord.

Despite the clear skies outside, the house has a gloomy, stormy feel. My father hasn't emerged from the bedroom since a group of jumpers deposited him here last night, reeking of whiskey and piss and cursing about how screwed up everything is: his life, his business, his rotten friend Paco, and me.

I made the list.

My stomach has been in knots since I heard him. I know

that's the moment I couldn't fall back asleep. I had to lie there with a tangled stomach and listen to them fight.

> *"She jumped today, Ayida. Did you know that? Snuck her stupid, crazy ass on the plane and jumped! I can command an entire unit of troops but not my own daughter."*
>
> *"Commanding never worked for her. You know that. She needs you. You can't hide behind the DZ. We are losing our daughter. She's been trying to get your approval her whole life. Does she have to die to do it? And if that happens, do you think that business is going to be enough to keep you from going over the edge?"*
>
> *"I haven't been to the edge in years."*
>
> *"You're drinking again. Every drink you have is another step closer. Why don't you get in command of yourself before you think you can command Ryan or anybody else for that matter?"*
>
> *"Out, bitch!"*

"Now, Mama," Ayida says, mixing mashed bananas into a bowl, "you haven't been feeling well at all and—"

"Did you *not* just call me Mama?" Gran's voice rattles in her island accent. "Don't talk to me like I'm the child here. I want to go to the mountains, to that lake we used to visit, and I'm going to go if I have to find a way to get there myself."

"This is sounding a lot like hitchhiking for pancakes," I mutter.

"Snitch!" Gran hollers at me.

"There is so much going on." My mom sighs, but Gran interrupts again.

"*Life* is going on, child. And for some of you, it's going to keep on going on, God willing. This world don't give a hot hoot how you spend your day. I don't think the Maker cares either, as long as you spend it with gratitude. Every problem you're baking bad bread about will still be here when we get back."

Gran inhales a long, careful breath like she's trying to net a butterfly and hold it to her chest. "Make an old lady happy," she entreats. "I want to go for a drive in the sunshine. I want to roll the windows down and let my gray hair fly in the breeze and listen to the music of the world humming by."

My mother and I look at each other in defeat. I mean, how do you say no to *that*?

Within the hour we are packed into the sedan with a cooler of drinks and foul-tasting baked goods. My father is noticeably absent, apparently feeling too much like he's on a winding road just lying in his bed. I don't want him here anyway.

Another hefty sigh escapes my mom, but from the back seat Gran smiles with satisfaction as we head off. As promised, she made me pull the silver pins from her hair so she could wear it loose around her shoulders. The result gives her a strangely girlish look, but that could also be from the unabashed glee of getting her way.

The arid desert yields to the mountain pass that rises steeply from the dry desert floor. A green vitality from yesterday's rain wafts in through the open windows. Soon we're rocking in that gravity-versus-weightless way you do when going around deep curves and switchbacks on a mountain road.

My brow creases with worry when I look at Gran. Her skin used to resemble a gleaming, oiled river rock. Now it's the flat color of a river rock left in the sun to dry. I instantly understand why she wanted to come up here when she's not feeling well. The mountains are *alive,* teeming with rich, dank life all around us. She wants to absorb it.

"I want to be there already and stick my fat black toes in the mud," Gran says.

"If we could go as the crow flies, we'd be there already," my mother answers, curving around another hairpin turn.

"I think it's funny how many animal sayings we have like that: as the crow flies . . ."

My mother tosses me an approving smile. She looks happy to finally have a light conversation. The meds must be kicking in: I feel blithe, carefree. "To have a bee in your bonnet."

"Bull in a china shop," I blurt.

"Monkey's uncle!" shouts Gran.

"It's raining cats and dogs!"

"It's raining men!" We all laugh together.

"Oooh, oooh, I've got one . . . I don't give a rat's ass," I add, earning a sideways look from my mother, but her smile is still bright, especially as she hears Gran give a mandatory disapproving cluck while stifling a giggle. "Remember that mangy cat, Sir Charles, that used to come around and leave gross *presents* at the door like he was bestowing us the greatest of offerings?" I'm laughing with the memory of stepping out too many times in bare feet onto something repulsive, like the tail of a mouse.

No one laughs with me, and even though Gran is blind, they exchange a look.

The skin over my mother's knuckles stretches a hair thinner as she clutches the wheel. "I . . . I don't remember that, honey."

Well, she has to be mistaken, because the memory surfaced clear and vivid, making my toes curl in reflexive disgust. I'm flung out of the joviality of the moment and into the black void of being the girl with the crazy thoughts. I don't understand. I remember the cat. I *remember*.

"Baby" — my mom pats my leg — "we're gonna come up on the lake after this turn. Describe it to your grandmother. You know she loves that."

The car swooshes around another bend and the mountain opens up, revealing a shimmering blue jewel in the valley of its hands. "The lake is below us, Gran, at the base of the cliffs we're driving on. With all the trees it's" — I search for the right description, wanting to paint it in her mind as beautifully as I'm seeing it — "it's like a sapphire hidden in grass."

Gran sighs and nods contentedly. She sees it now.

"Families are on the shore. Someone's throwing a stick in the water for a dog to fetch. People are diving off bubbles of gray rocks. Clouds are lazing about, and you can see them reflected in the lake." The truth is, it reminds me of her cloudy blind eyes, but I'm not sure if I should say that.

The moment I have that thought, the entire lake transforms below us, morphing and darkening into an enormous watchful eye in the mountain, with a deep black hole of a pupil in its center. Shivers prick my neck.

Echoing in my head are these words, a repetitive incantation, louder and louder . . .

This is the hole she crawls out of. This is the hole she crawls out of.

I scream, reach over, and jerk the steering wheel away from the enormous eye.

My mother startles and yanks the steering wheel back, swerving the car into the oncoming traffic. A horn blares loudly right in front of us as we swerve again, but too far, and we fishtail across the lanes back toward the jagged cliff and the enormous eye below. I scream and turn away from the window, not wanting to fall into that black hole where she waits for me.

Metallic screeches ring out as the side of the car swipes the guardrail. Another jerk to the right and we veer off the road on the opposite side, spinning, falling, and bouncing until we're stopped with a hard and thunderous bang.

All is silent.

TWENTY-FIVE

THE FIRST SOUND that filters in is the chirping of disturbed birds and a hissing sound that might be the radiator. My eyes blink heavily, but my chin feels connected to my chest, where a singular line of blood snakes its way from somewhere down my neck and onto my shirt. It's hard to lift my head. All my weight is forward, my body strains against the seat belt, and I realize we're facing downhill; mercifully, a large tree has stopped us from falling farther down the ravine.

Down to the eye.

Next to me, my mother groans. Her head rests on the steering wheel. Much more blood than I see on myself flows from her head, down her face like tears, and over her full lips. Her right forearm and wrist are bent at an odd angle. "Mom?" I'm afraid to touch her.

"Mom," she repeats. Thank God, she can hear me.

Then I realize ... she's heard my voice, she's found her own, so she's naturally reaching up the chain, grasping to know if her own mother is okay. I strain to turn around, pulling myself over the top of the seat back. Gran is folded in half, slumped against the door; the window has a spider's web of cracks in it. I call her name, struggle to reach and touch her, but she is still.

Calls bounce down to us from somewhere above through the trees. "Hang on! We're getting help!"

"Hurry!" I croak too quietly and try again. I don't see blood on my grandmother, but who knows the extent of her injuries.

I have an eternity to think about what happened.

We are the center of the universe, and the sun rotates around us as we wait for help. My mother is in and out of consciousness. I've cried out to Gran, tried to reach her, wherever she is, but the longer she's quiet, the more scared I become. She's withstood the pains and hardships of life longer than any of us, but her age makes her seem more fragile.

The girl who follows me may or may not be real. I was sure before that she was, but how can she be so big that the entire lake was one staring eye? That's not possible. Unless ... unless I really am schizophrenic, and the drugs haven't yet stomped down the illusions of my monstrous mind. All I know is that as we hang precariously on this slope, I realize that nearly everyone in my life has been hurt by me, or by her . . .

But it doesn't matter where I assign the blame. It's all hurt. And it's all me.

Is being alive worth it if you're nothing but a wrecking ball?

The sounds of sirens wind up the mountain, getting louder and louder until they are screeching right above us. A choir of voices discusses the best way to help us. Bless the man who reaches us first, looks in my eyes, and says, "We've got you now. It's gonna be okay."

I nod and cling to his words.

"They're here to help us, Ayida."

"You never used to call me by my name. I don't like it," she says — her voice is a crack of dry wood — and blacks out again.

Beginning with Gran, and then my mother, we are eventually all pulled from the mangled car and hauled up to the road, where ambulances whisk us off to the hospital. I have a gash in my neck where the seat belt cut into me, but I can sit up, and so I do, wrapped in a blanket, riding along with Gran. She's alive, the medic assures me of that, but still unconscious. Halfway down the mountain, my stomach heaves, and I throw up all over the floor.

"Am I dead yet?"

It's the most beautiful sound, Gran talking to me from her hospital bed. The nurse tells my mother that Gran's blood pressure is dangerously low.

"No," I answer, tears rising in my eyes. Guilt squeezes my throat closed. I did this. If I hadn't freaked out, we'd be winding back down the mountain, pleasantly tired after a day in the sun with the wind blowing in her gray hair. Not sitting in the hospital, where the smell of sickness makes me queasy.

"I never got to stick my toes in the mud."

I sniff. "I know. There's still time."

"No."

That word slams like gnarled hands on piano keys.

The beep of the heart-rate monitor keeps slow time.

"Instead of me singing my song, my song is singing to me." Gran's voice is a low, scratchy purr. "That's how I know it's time to go," she says. "It's calling me home."

From behind me, my mother sobs into one hand. The other hand is in a cast. Tears seep through her fingers like she's dipped her onyx palm into holy water. Her reaction tells me this is not just melodramatics. Gran isn't the type for that. If she says she's going to die, she is, and there's nothing any of us are going to do about it.

My father paces restlessly across the room. Helplessness strikes a chord of anguish in me. I feel like we're letting her die, and it's strangely familiar, like I've lived this moment before. My awful dreams becoming real. I close my eyes, afraid my muddled thoughts will summon the face again.

Ayida sits alongside Gran and strokes her face with her working hand. Gran accepts the loving touch with gratitude, already looking relieved to have announced her imminent departure. She's just broken every heart in the room, yet she looks peaceful.

"Tell me something true," she demands.

My mother bows her head reverently and thinks a moment before raising herself up proudly. "Your mothering has been solid and mystical. Mama, you've been my rock, you've been the clear waters at its edge, and you've been the deep mysteries of the darker waters. I thank you for sharing your life with me."

My father clears his throat. I have to look away from the glassy film of tears over his blue eyes. He clears his throat a second time. His legs are tented in a wide stance, like he needs help balancing. His hands are clasped low in front of him. "You've made me a better man."

Gran nods appreciatively. "Burn a cigar with my body, Nolan."

She inclines her head toward me, anticipating. I swallow hard. What do I tell her? I'm tortured? Screwed up? That I feel responsible for everything that's gone wrong since I was lying in this same hospital weeks ago?

What's true is that I don't know what's true.

Those things can't be the last thing she wants to hear from me. "Gran?" I start, with a slight tremor. "Do you think people want to hear the truth no matter what it is? When someone is dying, it seems you should say what will bring them peace."

Her weathered hand clasps my own. "That's how I know you're not yourself. I didn't always agree with you, child, but I trusted you because you spoke your truth no matter how untrue it was for the rest of us. No matter how foolish or headstrong you were being."

Does this mean she doesn't trust me now?

A wry laugh puffs from her chapped lips. "But God, you sure live the deep end of life's pool. That's something to respect." Ayida wipes her eyes. She gives me a sad, knowing smile as Gran talks to me. There's a long pause and a breath that seems to take more effort before Gran says, "My something true . . . you've got to live with integrity so you can die with integrity."

Tears stream down my face. A braided knot twists in my stomach. I desperately want Gran to stay with me. I want to tell her *all* my truths, even the ones that might turn her away. The scary and confusing things I'm seeing, the visions inside my head that have no continuity, how nothing matches up, as though the puzzle pieces of two lives got scrambled and don't fit together.

I'm the imagination of myself, like that paper said in the motor home.

Gran's blind, but she sees more than anyone else. Right now it feels like she's the only one who can help me.

My mouth opens to speak, but Gran doesn't just look like she has her eyes closed. Her face has lost its expectancy. My heart stutters. Has she . . . ?

Machines are still beeping, though. She's simply fallen asleep. Her chest rises and falls slowly. The pauses between exhale and inhale are excruciating. Every gap extends. I find myself holding my breath until she takes another one. My body taps into an inexplicable knowing of how it feels to have your breath come slower and slower until that last one becomes a boulder you can't push uphill anymore.

My dad falls wearily into a chair. My mom doesn't move from the bed, just sits there staring at Gran's face, her eyes replaying a lifetime of memories as she watches her sleep. We don't know if she'll ever wake again. Every so often, the corner of her mouth tips up into what might be a grin. I wonder if she's dreaming or revisiting her own memories.

Memories are so much like dreams.

An hour passes. Maybe more. We are all suspended, not wanting to leave for fear she will tiptoe out of life behind our backs.

"Now sing me your song again, Ryan," Gran whispers into the new night, startling my mother and me. My father was snoring softly a few feet away, but he wakes with a jolt at Gran's voice and the mention of my name. Soldiers half sleep like that.

"My song, Gran?"

She answers so low, we have to lean in to hear. "The one you were humming to me just now."

"It's okay. She's slipping away," my mother chokes out in answer to my confused expression. She leans in and kisses her mother, leaving tears on her cheek. Tenderly, she wipes it into Gran's skin. "It's okay to go, Mama. Nothing to be scared of. It will be beautiful there."

I'm sobbing. I can't help it.

"Yes, it's okay," Gran adds. "Ryan is waiting for me."

Everyone frowns and darts glances at me. Shivers roll over my mom's skin, making her head shake.

Gran's last breath is an exhale. It sounds like relief.

TWENTY-SIX

IT'S NEVER RIGHT to go to the hospital with four people and come home with three. Never.

A scream: *It's your fault!*

Rattled to my bones, I yelp and stumble into Nolan's side, and he looks at me like he wants to shove me across the room far away from him. His eyes are as accusatory as the voice. I don't know if it's the girl, who's been abnormally quiet since our accident. It has her anger but feels more intimate. Like another part of me. My throat constricts with the tears I'm trying to hold back.

Wordless, everyone disperses with heads down to their own corners of the house. I go to my room and find myself staring at the white walls, the pinholes where the lights used to hang above my bed, the books on the shelves, and scrapbooks of pictures, which I hadn't realized were tucked in with the books. Odd that I'd forget the scrapbooks were there, but I see now that there is one for each year. Yes, Joe and I made these together every summer.

Until this summer.

Life came to a halt this summer.

I flip through the years of us: me and JoeLo. God, our friendship was beautiful. I can see it in the way we make the same expressions. The way our bodies lean into each other with such comfort. We are brother and sister. Were . . .

My heart hurts.

Live with integrity; die with integrity.

Joe went and spoke to Dom after we fought. Proof of love. I need to apologize to him.

Dom's origami tiger watches me from the dresser as I flip through the pages of another life. The paper tiger was supposed to be a message. I thought I understood the message when I decided to jump. But maybe Dom intended for me to hear a different roar. I pick it up. The delicate brush-strokes of paint speak their own message: that Dom cared enough about me to painstakingly make a reminder of how he sees me.

Saw me.

Could there be a message written inside? It seems a shame to ruin the tiger to find out. We stare at each other, this tiger and I.

I rip it in half.

Tumbling from its belly is a small memory card. The rumble in my chest is unwelcome—I don't know anymore if it's the girl who disturbs me or my own broken mind, but I do my best to ignore the feeling of eyes on me. I put the memory card into the laptop on my desk and press play.

Dom's deep voice fills the room.

Dear Ryan, I made you this video to remind you of who I see every time I close my eyes. Who I dream of at night. Who I miss. You . . . in all your wild glory. You are the most beautiful creation.

Never have I seen myself like this. A candid picture of me walking with my chute crumpled against my chest after a jump, a mass of ringlets, and a mass of attitude. No one is in the picture with me, but I'm smiling. I appear to be smiling to myself, giddy with an inside joke about how badass life is. A picture of me and my mother, belly laughing. Our smiles are the same. A side shot of me giving the bare ass to my father with his back turned to me as he briefs a bunch of his boys before a jump. The smile on their faces says it all. The first sergeant has momentarily lost their attention.

The memory of this thought rushes in: *Now he knows how I feel.*

These are all pictures of me, but . . .

Babe, I love strong women. Hell, I was raised by one.
And now both of my strong women are gone. I'd
give anything to go backwards and erase that night in
the motor home. Everything changed that night. You
changed that night. Does it have to be forever?

The skydive calendar proofs scroll by. I gawk at the brazen images, feeling disassociated, like the girl I see is so completely foreign to me, I can't even say she's me.

It is no longer *me* but *her*.

Her with her cola skin, her full lips sauced with shimmering gloss, and her skintight red skydive jumpsuit unzipped down her ridged belly. Everything in her cat eyes says she's blatantly unafraid of being looked at, of showing the world exactly who she thinks she is.

She. Is. Unafraid.

Being unafraid of experience is what made you
extraordinary.

On top of a mountain. Her naked body is a silhouette, a dark S of curves against the night sky. Wind blows her puff of wild hair, licks her skin. A lightning storm rages and strikes out in the distance in front of her. Arms overhead, she is powerful: it's as though she can shoot lightning straight from her soul and out through her fingers. Watching her, I've no doubt she can.

Video now, of different jumps. Dom wears a camera on his jump helmet, flying toward me, *her*, floating in the sky; wind makes her cheeks ripple like water. She zooms closer, reaches for him with muscled arms in a tank top, and kisses him in freefall. Does everyone fall to the earth with such peace? Does everyone look so radiant after a kiss?

There are video clips of multiways of synchronized jumpers. I feel like God watching from above. It's a dance in the air. A colorful snowflake falling to earth. I'm in awe. And confusion. I'm watching superheroes. Do these people know how special they are? How dynamically alive and rare they are?

One jump is filmed from the ground. I hear Dom behind the camera, talking to someone next to him, excited anticipation and pride evident in his voice. One by one, parachutes burst open. The camera zooms out, then in, trying to focus on a dot of color hurtling toward the ground.

Falling so fast.

Falling.

Then, my father's voice: "Open, baby. Open, goddamn it.

Jesus, Ryan, don't do this to me . . . open the damn chute."
Hearing such anguish fills my eyes with tears. "I love you,
Ryan, please . . ."

He's never said that to me.

My eyes are glued to the screen. There is no way that
chute is going to open. I know who I'm watching, and
somewhere inside, the memory is there, but it's like watching a movie of my own death.

Her death.

My whole body vibrates in terrified anticipation as she
plummets toward packed dirt. My hands cover my mouth.
I'm pleading with her now, like her father, to please pull. I
want to look away, but I can't.

I'm watching my life flash before my eyes.

In an exhalation of color, the chute gusts open just in
time to catch her before she tumbles to the sandy ground.
Dom yells out and runs, the desert floor bouncing by on-
screen. I dread what he's about to see, until I realize the
camera has stopped moving and is pointed at the smiling
face of the girl who haunts me in every reflection. She's
holding something toward the camera.

"The penny, bitches!"

For the first time, I really see what everyone else sees. No
wonder they miss the old Ryan. No wonder they want her

back. That Ryan *was* larger than life. I've tried to be that Ryan, but it's like she's died in me. She deserves to live on. I don't know whose side I'm on anymore: mine, or . . . mine?

In a daze, I wander to Gran's empty room. It smells like her: warm skin, strange medicinal creams, cigar smoke. Magic.

I feel her.

Her soft, aged skin in the bath water. Her wrinkled hands, limber only on the piano. Her blind eyes, which saw through me. She was magic. I'm so privileged to have known her.

I realize I can't think of her proper name. This baffles me. How can I not remember my grandmother's name?

The Obeah religion Gran practiced was a lot of the "dark water" my mother spoke about. Unknowable, mysterious. She probably made much of it up. I think Gran was her own religion. Her philosophy of life and death rings true, though.

Live with integrity. Die with integrity.

If you don't do one right, you can never do the other right.

Wishing I could use magic to rectify things, I finger the objects of her altar. Placed around a creamy hand-spun bowl are a shell filled with cigar ashes, feathers from various birds that look like they died in a fiery crash, and four flat, smooth stones that feel as solid as vows when I press them into my palm.

I light a half-burned stick of incense and walk to the freestanding antique mirror that's in the corner of the room, between two windows. Smoke curls up into the air behind me.

I lean toward the mirror. The old glass ripples my image. Flecks of black paint shadow the glint in the glass. Shafts of moonlight slice through the night air and land at my feet. I'm so tired, my heart is sagging against restraints in my chest.

She's been chasing me for weeks, filling my head with strange words and memories. I'm ready to be done with our battle. I'm exhausted. I want to step into the light with Gran. My palms press against the cool glass of the mirror as I stare into myself, willing Death to come. Closer and closer, I inch my face to my reflection, until my forehead knocks against itself.

This feels familiar, this pressing my face against the glass, this longing to merge with something larger than myself.

This is how we found each other.

I whisper against my own lips, "Come and get me."

TWENTY-SEVEN

NOTHING HAPPENS. This is more startling, now that I've requested her presence, than seeing her face would be. I pull back, angry.

"Did you hear me? I give up! Come for me!"

The glass vibrates under my fists. "I don't want to live this life anymore. Do what you're going to do and quit playing with me." A sob escapes. "I give up." I'm angry at myself for thinking it, saying it, but it's true. Everything is wrong. Everything.

I saw who I used to be. Like everyone else, I'm mourning the spark of that person. I'm not her. I'll never be her.

Death is after me, speaks to me, watches me. She took Gran. Who will be next if I don't let her win? Why not submit?

Death always gets her way in the end.

TWENTY-EiGHT

THE SHADOW OF Gran's head indents her pillow.

Strange, the shadows we leave behind.

I've stared at it so long, the sun has risen and set on its wrinkled surface. The sun rises and sets on everything. On every life. When the last shaft of golden light tiptoes away from her bed, I crawl into it. I want sleep, the dark kind. I want to never wake up. Gran's sweet, old smell envelops me as I burrow into the covers and wrap myself in silence.

Night comes. Day passes. The earth tosses and turns in its big black bed.

Black morning.   Black mourning.

I hear whisperings. They drift in and out like oysters opening and closing in the current.

"We should call the doc."

"Depression?"

"It's been two days."

"This is what heartbreak looks like. She loved her grandmother."

"This is scaring me."

I want to tell them I love them before I'm gone, but love is stuck like a pearl in my closed heart.

TWENTY-NiNE

I dreamed I was somebody else.

I wake, and still I feel like somebody else.

Both lives equally real.

Both lives equally dreamlike.

Clear water and deep water.

Not fully rested, not fully awake, I'm tired down to my soul.

I figure that today is a good day to

                              fall.

THIRTY

THE JOURNAL SITS on my lap, and I snap it closed. I said once that nothing is more fun than to give Death the finger and have fun while you're doing it. But Death's a relentless hag. When you cheat Death of its prize, it keeps coming after you. Death never forgets a debt. Those eyes will follow me everywhere. Always.

This is no life.

The destructive force I've become to the people around me makes *me* a reaper. There's only one way to stop it. I have to face the fact that I wasn't supposed to live.

I have to right the wrong. So much of me has already died. Why not give up the rest?

The few final notes I scribble into my journal aren't supposed to be a goodbye, though I realize that anything I write will read like one. I wish I could take away the only question they will have afterward, but *Why?* isn't the right question. *How?* will be self-explanatory. The right question is *What?* What happened? What *really* happened to the girl we used to call Ryan Poitier Sharpe? I tried to tell them I wasn't mentally ill. I tried to tell them I was being haunted. If anything drove me crazy, it was that.

And not being believed.

Doubt is a chain-rattling ghost.

THIRTY-ONE

THE DESERT WIND is so hot, I feel like the devil is breathing on me. My body isn't working right. It's uncooperative. Slow movements, fumbling with buttons and zippers, struggling to clip my parachute chest strap. It's built to snap together, but it's like the clips are opposing magnets, resisting. Finally I force them together and get the pack secured. There's a fleeting thought that I shouldn't bother with a parachute. What's the point? But then they wouldn't let me on the plane, would they?

I have to get on the plane. There are lots of ways to die, but this is so right, it's poetic.

The drop zone is a hive. People dart in and out, worker bees and drones ready for flight. Excitement is a thing you can feel here. It's a sugary syrup over the beige of the Mojave. With the big-way and the site visit from the X Games people later in the afternoon, it's the only day busy enough for me to get in the air without trouble. I'm just another drone. I'll get on the plane, and when I jump, I'll track my body as far away from the DZ as I can so they won't see. They won't have to find me. I'll come to rest in the harsh, beautiful, unforgiving desert.

Ashes to ashes. Dust to dust.

We all get on the airplane. My eyes meet the exhilarated eyes of a familiar guy. Only skydivers look exhilarated at eight a.m. He flicks a thumbs-up at me with maniacal happiness, and that's when I see him in memory . . . Birthday Boy. I teased him one day, scared him for fun. Then I blew him a kiss as I fell out of the plane. I guess he came back for more.

My father once said, *You don't become a part of the skydiving life. Skydiving becomes part of you. Some people do it once, to say they did. Others do it and realize they were living a half life before that and they'll only feel alive on the edge.*

Half life. That best describes mine. It isn't enough of a life.

Birthday Boy looks at me quizzically, and I turn my head toward the wall of the plane, focus on the dots of rivets holding the aluminum panels together. "Scared?" he asks.

"No," I answer. "I've done this before."

Only I know we're not talking about the same thing.

The wind skims through the cabin; the air slapping our faces makes it real. I think I hear a song riding on its currents. It feels good to hum, to feel the vibration of my voice, so I do. But once I start, I can't stop. This song rises from a deeper part of me than my self-control.

My song.

"Siren," I say. "Of course you're with me now."

I'll never leave.

"You don't have to sing to me. I'm already yours."

My song! she yells in my head.

Someone opens the jump door. The spotter signals the pilot, and the plane powers down. Everyone stands. I rise to my feet.

Birthday Boy places a gentle hand on my arm. "You're talking to yourself," he says, then looks at me closer. "I recognize you. From my first jump. You seem . . . *different.*"

We stare at each other. This stranger's concern is a rope. I can't afford to let him lasso me and reel me back in. "You okay? Maybe sit this one out?" he asks.

I shake my head. "I'm all in." My heart thuds wildly as I lumber behind the other jumpers toward the open door of the plane. The song pounds so loud in my head, it hurts. I can't shut it out. Only one way to stop it. I'll go to the silence again.

Birthday Boy enters the doorway, poised to jump, but

stops, holds himself from falling. Both arms are stretched out to each side of the open door. He looks back at me through his goggles with questions swarming his eyes. The wordless moment that passes between us is spoken in one of the most beautiful languages in human history.

I force a smile through trembling lips and blow him a kiss, and he's gone. Later I will be one of his regrets. He will wonder if he should have done more. That makes me sad.

One by one, jumpers take to the sky like dandelion seeds swept away on their own wishes. I wonder about their wishes.

I have the wish to die.

THIRTY-TWO

I HEARD MY SONG!

Finally.

Heard the strong, tender melody in the stillness of the void. It kept me anchored to my body. Carried me back to myself whenever I felt the urge to drift into the light. The urge was never stronger than when Gran took my hand in that dark place. I sang to her a lot. With her sad, now-seeing eyes, she beckoned me to come with her. "Walk with me toward the love," she said.

It was so tempting.

But instead I chose to watch her go to another place so I could stay in the dark and bang on the glass of my own life.

Watch, while someone else lived it.

Now she wants to end it.

I have to stop her.

I have the wish to live.

THiRTY-THREE

THE BLASTING SOUND of wind and the drone of the engines fade the minute I step into the doorway. All I can hear is my raging heartbeat and the relentless song ringing in my temples. My toes hang off the edge of the opening. My jumpsuit presses to my shins and arms as I lean forward.

Ashes to ashes. Dust to dust.

The earth is waiting to fold me back into itself.

I smile as I roll and plummet through the air in a tumbling heap. I'm leaping into her arms. She finally wins.

Hurtling through the air, I'm letting gravity wrap its hand around me and suck me down. Tracking away from the bare circle of the drop zone, I'm cloaked in a fear like I've never known. I'm trying to surrender. I'm letting go.

We fought once and I lost. I won't lose again. It's on!

Her fear and her surrender are the footholds I need.

She may have my body, but I've got something she doesn't—fear-lessness.

I am stronger than her fear. She's willing to die, and she's freaking terrified. That releases her hold on my body just enough to allow me back in.

Barely.

I'm no longer her specter. I'm her shadow, part of her, part of myself again.

I can feel the warm wind on my lips, and it's the most delicious taste.

I want more.

I want control of my body. I want to reclaim it. I want to dance on the currents again. I want to taste warm mint on Dom's tongue, feel raucous laughter shake me as it does when Joe and I joke around, know again the spoonful of spiked sugar that is sex, the sensual chill of skinny-dipping in the reservoir, the sweetness of my mother's hugs.

I want my life back.

And I'll be goddamned if this bitch is going to take it forever.

I don't understand what's happening. The voice that was singing in my head as I exited the plane is now pushing out of my mouth. I'm falling, and I'm humming a song.

—

My song. I'll choke her with it. I'm not just singing the music; I am the music: as physical yet ephemeral as a tune floating on the wind. Real, but existing as a cluster of vibrations, somehow getting stronger and stronger, pulsing with life, until I have the power to break through.

The wind tries to stuff the tune back in my mouth. Ground rushes up to meet me, and I curl in on myself. I can do this. I can die. But I can't go back in the womb without wrapping around myself, making myself smaller.

She cannot roll into a ball. She's making my body a dark, round stone. I try to push harder into the shell of me, assert my ownership, take control of my body so I can stabilize the fall, stop her from killing me.

Again.

This time it'll be permanent.

Please, no. If she takes my body, I'll have no home to return to.

I concentrate, visualize my spirit as a vapor seeping into every cell, every long strand of marrow, the tiniest corners of nerves. I push harder than I've ever pushed for anything.

Let. Me. In!

My fingers twitch uncontrollably against my chest strap. My hands fling away from my body. The air is trying to pull me apart—to prohibit my arms from crossing over my chest—to spread me wide like a bird. My body is making spastic movements. My eyes spring open, and I see the one thing I don't want to see: the multicolored patchwork of earth below growing larger. It won't be long before impact.

Death already has a hold of me now; I feel her, asserting her power, trying to take my body prematurely, like she can't wait until I die. She wants to take me alive. I fight to tug my body back into a ball, but I'm like a spring that tries to uncoil to a safe position.

Anger flows through me. My eyes are pinned open. She won't let me close them and fall oblivious to the exact moment of impact. She wants to torture me, make me watch. Involuntarily, my body tracks back over the drop-zone area. She wants to make them watch too. Cruel.

I force my eyes closed.

I think I have her now. I'm in, partially directing my arms and legs, stretching my body into an arch, tracking away from the enormous, flat desert. It hurts, though. After weeks of expansive floating in spirit form, I feel gravity like an iron anvil strapped to every bone.

She's fighting my will, trying to curl up like the tandem jumpers who panic in freefall. Dom had to head-butt a guy once, knock him out cold, so that he wouldn't keep grabbing Dom's hands and kill them both. *God, I've missed him so much . . .*

I've missed everyone. Everything.

Rushing through me are anger and the heat of longing to live. I have to want to live more than she wants to die. But our altitude is so low, and I can't seem to inhabit my body powerfully enough to pull the chute. Panic sets in, foreign and unwelcome.

The spirit, the fucking thief, thinks she can freaking close her eyes and wait to bounce.

Any second now, it will be over. Any second . . .

I know something she doesn't know. It's the only thing keeping me from giving up as I hear screams from the drop zone below.

I've been here before.

I know how far I can fall before it's too late.

Relax, I tell myself. Wait for the release. This will be your freedom. I start to mumble a prayer. I don't know where this prayer comes from, but it bubbles up like so many other disconnected memories. I try to mumble the prayer and wait to hit the ground, but that damn song is all that comes out.

I'm screaming my song, and it's my voice, my shaky voice. If I can't get a firm grip on my body, make my arms and hands work right, if I can't pull the ripcord in a matter of seconds, I'm going to die. I'm going to walk into that light.

That's going to piss me off so much.

Oh God.
Now.

Oh God.
Now.

THiRTY-FOUR

Piercing screams reverberate, bouncing off the Sierra Nevada, bouncing off the needles of cacti, out into the desert and back—a boomerang of shrieks and pain. A final heartbreaking gust of wind, and multicolored strips of nylon flutter ineffectively.

I fly out of my body on impact, sent hurtling through the air and the mirage-like veil that undulates between life and death. I am that one reckless balloon streaming toward the blue skies.

Hovering above, I look across the desert at the gnarled and twisted shapes of the cacti. I look down at my gnarled and twisted body. Suddenly I am on the ground, just feet away from my physical self. I look so small . . .

People are running, scurrying like ants toward my still form. Dad falls to his knees beside me. Love wafts from him in a kaleidoscope of colors as he bends over me. He's still the first sergeant, shouting orders to people. *Call an ambulance. Don't touch her. My baby. My baby.*

I finally see his love. Like Gran, I can see so clearly now that I'm gone. I had to die to see it? This strikes me as incredibly sad.

A timid voice carries across the sand to me. "Are . . . are you the Angel of Death?"

I don't know this girl, but she floats nearby, concern and confusion evident in her crystalline blue eyes. I've seen those eyes before. Her blond hair lifts and falls like she's in water. She looks so sad, but she scares me too. I don't want any spirits nearby, coaxing me into the light.

I want to live. It's all I've ever wanted.

"You're the one who's been haunting me," she says, wide-eyed. "You died and—"

"I'm not dead!"

Maybe I am, I realize, looking at my broken body. My father's mouth is locked over mine. He blows. Pumps his palms on my chest. Listens for breath. Cries. I wish I could feel his tears, which run down his cheeks and pink my dusty lips.

I'm afraid to look at the crowd. I can't bear to see Dom's luminous spirit crushed. I can't bear to see my mother's wailing black grief. There's no more wind. It's like the world is holding its breath to see if I'll make it. But, I realize sadly, the world is used to this. The comings and goings of humans is old news. What I'm feeling is the stillness of not being alive anymore.

I *was* alive. This was my life.

Anger and sadness are a hook knife ripping through my soul. The stronger my emotions, the more I'm pulled toward my physical form. She moves closer too, and when I look in her eyes, I realize with a gasp . . . it's *her*. This skinny scrap of teenage girl is the spirit who stole my life from me. I remember the first time I looked into her eyes in the motor home.

I turn away from my father and his resuscitation attempts. "What did you think you were doing?" I'm torn between flying through her and breaking her into a million points of light, or staying with myself, with Dad, as he cries and fights to save me. I desperately want to stay until I can't stay any longer.

"I — I was living my life."

"You were living *my* life!"

The spirit moves between me and my body. She inclines her head and holds her hands up like an angelic statue. She looks like she's thinking very hard about something, concentrating, before her eyes open wide. She looks at my body, looks down at her skin. "That's not me. Oh, God. I remember now."

"What? What do you remember?"

"I was sick. I . . . I had *cancer*." There's bite to that last word. "My parents denied me medical care after I was diagnosed. 'God's will,' my father called it. If we prayed, if we were faithful enough, God would spare me. I tried to believe they were right. I was supposed to honor them, right? But I didn't." Her voice goes hard. "Secretly, I hated them. They wouldn't give me the morphine. They wanted me to suffer. My father said my pain would purify me. They drove me out to nowhere in that motor home and let me die."

The girl looks out on the horizon, and I know her body is out there, somewhere.

"I couldn't leave, though. It wasn't fair. I wanted to live. But I was stuck in this dark, lonely place."

I know that dark place. Her story is sad. It is.

"Suddenly, there you were," she continues, her words rushing out. "So beautifully alive. From that first moment I saw you, I somehow connected with you, followed you. I couldn't stop watching you, but you were so arrogant about life. You didn't seem to care whether you had it or not. I was angry that you had a choice and risked what I wanted more than anything. You flirted with death, dared it. When you came back to the motor home and fell into the glass, I somehow fell into you, into *life* again."

"How could you take my life?" I demand. "How dare you think you could *be* me?"

Her eyes take on a helpless grief. "I thought I'd been given a second chance. You tossed your life at my feet!"

The wails of sirens scream in the background. My dad hears them too. He looks up at the sky, looks at his watch.

We're running out of time.

He hasn't given up fighting for my life. I wonder how that makes her feel. It makes me feel gratitude. Hope. And it makes me very sad.

She moves closer, inches from me. "There's forgetfulness when you're reborn. I had memories of my" — she pats her slender chest — "*my* real life. I see that now. But they were unclear. Like a dream. So confusing. I started journaling about it. I knew I'd come back from death, but I didn't know why everything felt so strange, unfamiliar. I had memories of two lives: foggy scraps of mine, from before . . . and the mirage of your life." She taps her head. "I had all your memories. Only I couldn't feel any attachment to them. I was numb. Everyone said I was crazy. I thought you were hunting me because I — you — were supposed to die the night of the LSD." Her eyes go wide and she covers her mouth. "It was *my* house I ran to from the doctor's office. It was *my* own dead body I saw in my mind. I was trying to remember myself."

She wore my body like a new dress, and screwed up my relationships, and tried to kill me. Or kill herself. It's a mindfuck. But strangely, I find compassion rising within me for this girl who died because her parents didn't fight for her.

"No one will be waiting for me," she says, sounding so alone. So scared.

"Gran will." Without a doubt, I know that Gran won't let this girl journey alone. She won't let either of us go alone into the light.

We stand, silent for a moment.

"I wasn't haunting you, Rachel," I say, remembering with sudden clarity her name from the back of the maroon Bible. Her eyes fly open as the name leaves my lips, and I know I'm right. "I was following you. I was desperately fighting for my own life!"

I think back to the night of the LSD trip. "What I did was stupid," I admit, regretfully. "I let you in. But I tried to get back. I clung to my body, to my life. I tried to let people know not to trust you." I recall the kiss with Joe. How I pushed so hard for her to kiss him so he'd know she couldn't possibly be me. But instead I only hurt him. I see that now. "You cut my hair off . . ." It seems like a stupid thing to say.

The spirit ventures closer to me, but not in a threatening way: beseeching, her eyes seeking forgiveness. "I didn't know it was you in the reflections. I thought it was a ghost trying to possess me. But the ghost had the same reflection I saw every day in the mirror. I didn't know how to stop it, but I knew I was ruining my life." She pauses, eyes to the ground. "*Your* life," she corrects. "I couldn't live like that. People were suffering. I realized that Gran was right: a life without integrity isn't worth living at all."

"I would never give up on life. No matter how bad things were. Never!"

With those words I become a dark dandelion seed, furiously picked up and whipped in the wind.

Planted.

THIRTY-FIVE

SEARING PAIN IS the first thing I feel. It's hard to breathe. I try to move my legs. More pain floats through my body than blood. I'm steeping in it. Someone takes my hand, and I struggle to open my eyes. It's Daddy. His eyes are swollen from crying, but unabashed love shines from them. How could I have been so blind? Mom moves to kiss my cheek and stands next to him. They look down on me with such gratefulness. They sob, they laugh, relieved.

Joe and Dom are both wrinkled and sound asleep on worn chairs next to each other, like two mismatched brothers. It's one of the sweetest things I've ever seen.

Looking around the hospital room, I have a stab of panic wondering if any of it really happened. Maybe there *was* no sad-eyed girl in the desert with me. Maybe I never left the hospital from the LSD. Could it all have been a dream?

Could I be crazy after all?

If all of it *did* happen, my life is wreckage. There is so much to repair. Some damage might be permanent. Hurricane Crazy Girl debris. Relationships shattered, Gran dead, Dad's business in ruins.

How can I even tell them the truth? They'd think it was more ramblings from a nutjob. I wonder if I can find Rachel's journal . . .

At least Gran finally knew the truth. Now I know what she meant about my song. It's the most important tune you'll ever dance to: your *life* is your song. And the melody is how you live it. Each of us is a movement in the great symphony. I want to tell everyone this.

Live with integrity so you can die with integrity. Don't die without sharing your song.

Only through dying have I come to know what a gift it is to be alive. But they'll never believe me. I close my eyes. Hot tears run down to my temples. They think I tried to kill myself.

If they only knew how badly I tried to save myself.

When I was floating, I had the pain of watching someone else try to be me, and I could only throw my spirit against the door of my own life, desperate to break through. I think that emotional pain was worse than the pain I'm feeling now. I'll take this.

I'm the only one who can be me.

At one time I told Avery I'd rather be crazy and fully alive than sane and half-dead. I thought that nothing I did mattered. I was so full of shit. Half-dead sucks ass, half-dead hurts, but it's *life*. Now I realize: life is worth living, even when it hurts.

I might not have known that if it hadn't been taken away.

"I love you," I tell my parents. I roll my head sideways and see a message written in messy handwriting, lying on the table next to me. I wince as I reach with my one good hand to pick it up.

Your reflection is your own.

I point to the note with a hammering heart. "Who—who wrote this?"

My mother flashes me a perplexed, sympathetic look and lays her hand reassuringly over mine. "Honey ... *you* did."

ACKNOWLEDGMENTS

Yes, I flung myself out of perfectly good airplanes! I sucked at it, quite honestly. My fellow skydivers told me it was because my right ear sticks out more than my left, contributing to my tendency to turn constantly in freefall. I was a human with a bad rudder and only jumped thirty-nine times. But I'm still here, so by that measure of skydiving achievement, I guess I did well!

Thank you to the motley bunch of personalities who used to jump with me in California City back in 1993–94. Particularly, I wish to thank the Celaya family. I thought of Dennis often during the writing of this book and recall the days in the desert with all of you as some of the most memorable of my life.

As always, I must thank my distinguished (and by that I mean he's legendary, like *whoa*) and exceptional agent, Michael Bourret. Michael, I consider the day we decided to work together as one of the luckiest of my career. Thank you for your hard work and continued belief in me.

Much gratitude goes to my editor, Karen Grove. We've walked this path together four times now, and each time, I learn something new from you. Thank you for your love of my stories and careful attention to making them better. Working with you is an absolute joy.

Sydney and Cooper, you both are so brave, each in your own way. I hope you always feel bold enough to challenge any limiting fears. Thank you for always being behind me as I challenge mine.

Beta readers are so valuable, and I was lucky enough to have a few very talented people read the first draft of this book and help me improve it. I'm indebted to Tessa Elwood, Stephanie Kuehn, Heather Petty, Brent Watson, and Cheri Williams. The fact that I finally managed to really impress my crit partner, Heather, is a particular triumph. Love you, girl.

Thank you to my Tribe: Mary Claire, Lucy, and Jo — first readers who always ask for more and first friends who see me in all my complicated glory and still come back for more. I love you.

To Jason: You're an incredible example of facing fears and overcoming them. I'm so glad to have you with me on this wild ride and to know that while I *can* face things alone, I don't have to. It's just more fun to jump together.

On a serious but most vital note: You've just read a story where characters struggle with life-and-death choices. Dear reader, I know that some of you struggle too. *Please* know that you are not alone and that there are people who can help you. As Ryan would say, "Don't let a mongrel like fear back you down." There's always a way through the fires that test you. But if you find that impossible to believe right now, please call the National Suicide Prevention Hotline at 1–800–273–8255.

Love and blue skies to everyone!